EDGE OF THE WIND

EDGE OF THE WIND

James E. Cherry

STEPHEN F. AUSTIN STATE UNIVERSITY PRESS
2016

For more information:
Stephen F. Austin State University Press
P.O. Box 13007 SFA Station
Nacogdoches, Texas 75962
sfapress@sfasu.edu
www.sfasu.edu/sfapress

Book design: Shaina Hawkins
Distributed by Texas A&M Consortium
www.tamupress.com

LIBRARY OF CONGRESS CATALOGING-IN-PUBLICA-
TION DATA
Cherry James, E.
Edge of the Wind/James E. Cherry

ISBN: 978-1-62288-140-6

We are all apprentices in a craft where no one ever becomes a master.

~Ernest Hemingway

1

Alexander van der Pool awoke like a man crawling out of a deep dark hole. He yawned, stretched, rubbed crusts of sleep from his eyes and flipped off the radio that crackled with more static than jazz. The weather had changed since he'd been holed up in his sister's spare bedroom in Stovall, the middle of nowhere. Late September descended upon west Tennessee, blanketed it in shorter days, cooler temps. He knew that meant the frenzy of high school football, bright lights at the county fair and fields woven with intricate designs of cotton. Alex knew this part of the country well and hated it. He was born and raised in Stovall and couldn't believe after all these years he was now back where he started.

He blinked twice and everything sharpened into focus: four pairs of pants clung to the back of a chair, three short sleeved shirts draped a dresser. Several torn out pages from a legal pad haphazardly covered the bed. Books—poetry, novels, textbooks—were strewn across the bedroom floor as if nothing more than an afterthought. Some were dog-eared, others lay open on their bellies and many were stacked upon one another, but all were the by-product of his sister's four years at State College. In the last two months, Alex had read everything in the room, had re-read Dickenson, Langston Hughes, Hemingway, and Steinbeck, but he fell asleep with Richard Wright's *Native Son* across his chest. He groped like a blind man for the book beside him and when he did, it thudded against the floor.

Alex bolted upright, sat aside the bed, jerked his head around as if someone had called his name and he couldn't determine which direction it came from. He held *Native Son* like a rosary while his eyes settled on a photograph of himself, his sister and mother on the dresser. The image was as fresh as it was seventeen years ago. He closed his eyes and savored memory as if it were a slice of deep rich chocolate. He was nine years old, his sister Margaret, fourteen and their Mom between them with her arms draped around their shoulders. It was Saturday on an April afternoon and he was happy. Again. The three of them smiled as if Marshall Park was heaven and they had halos over their heads. Happy. He and his sister ran for the swing set, used their legs to break the bonds of gravity and raced toward the sun. Her legs were longer and stronger and sometimes she sailed so high and wide, he thought she would orbit the planet at any moment. The basketball court was another matter. What he lacked in height and length, he compensated for with speed and quickness. Alex faked left and drove right to get around Margaret and lay the ball off the backboard and through the net every time. Afterwards, his mother returned from their car, stretched a blanket across green grass down by the lake and the three of them bowed their heads and blessed a picnic basket of fried chicken, potato salad, fruit, and slices of chocolate cake. They washed it down cold bottles of orange soda and smacked their lips. His mother became recumbent against the earth, used an open book to shield her eyes from the sun. Margaret waved at a classmate, Elise, met her halfway to discuss Mrs. Sutherland's English class and Everett Bond who sat in the third row. Alex meandered by the lake, the late afternoon light warm and ethereal upon the water. He walked down a pier where kids his age used it as a diving board to splash in and out of the water, their laughter yellow and round as it bounced across the park. The wind rolled off of the day like a bedtime lullaby and no amount noise could drown out its sweet harmonies. He sat on the bank of the lake, lingered in the peace he'd found there. When he walked back towards his mom, four ducks flapped their wings and waddled after him. Alex felt bad that he had nothing to offer them and they soon stopped, watched him stumble up a hill. When he reached his mother and sister, Elise had joined them and was holding his mother's camera. He still remembered the inflection in Elise's voice when she said: "say cheese."

His mother and sister were all he'd had and all he'd needed. Before he was nine, there was a father in the house, but when he left, Alex, his sister, and his mother, stretched the fabric of their own lives to cover the hole and make the pattern complete again. The only thing that he possessed that belonged to his father was his last name and an old photograph. Most days he even managed to push those out of his mind. His sister and his mother were the only family he'd ever known and loved. It was as if he was born at nine years age. Anything before that time was too painful to remember.

Alex lay on his back with an open book across his chest, rolled his eyes towards the ceiling and watched his childhood in Stovall descend, light upon him. He wasn't raised in the rural part of the county like where his sister lived now. They lived in the middle of Cartmell Street with a Baptist church on one end and Berry Courts Housing Projects on the other. Wednesday nights and Sunday mornings, his mom led him by the hand to the house of the Lord where he attended Sunday school, sang in the youth choir, and was a junior usher. But Monday through Saturday the streets tugged at his shirtsleeve: fast-tailed girls agreed to show him theirs if he showed them his, fifty bucks was easy money just to look out for the police and kids his age or younger were already drinking and carrying guns. When he was a teenager, the BC's ruled the block and in order to walk that end of the street without getting a daily beat down, you had to pay a tax: join the gang. Alex was about to pay up one day when he was cornered by two of them after school. The one wearing an undershirt with a purple bandana tied around cornrows pinned his arms behind his back while the other, dripping gold chains from his neck, snarled a mouthful of invectives and gold teeth. He slapped Alex, took target practice on his navel with his fists. Alex doubled over and when he looked up from his knees, his sister Margaret, had high-heeled shoes in both hands and wailed away at everybody that didn't look like him. She invited them to join the van der Pool gang as they scampered away rubbing the knots on their head. She pulled Alex to his feet, admonished him for crying. Alex stayed away from that end of the street and the gangbangers stayed away from his big sister who vowed that when she got older she was going to find her some land in the country where she wouldn't have to fight for the sake of fighting. A good pair of stilettos were too expensive to get repaired every other day.

By his junior year in high school, Alex played end on the football team and caught two touchdowns against Farragut. After the game, he waited at the kitchen table for his mom to come home to share the news. She willed herself through the door and he didn't recognize her. She aged ten years since leaving home that morning. Her hair had grayed. Lines formed around her eyes and her shoulders drooped from working as an elementary school secretary by day and cleaning offices at night. He rushed from his chair, helped her remove her coat and kissed her on the jaw. He wished her a goodnight and she replied that she loved him as she dragged herself to bed. The next day Alex quit the football team and got a job bagging groceries after school at the Piggly Wiggly. He thought about quitting school altogether to work full time, but Mom threatened to break his left leg and Margaret, away at college, his right if he did so.

His senior year started great. Mom didn't have to scrub toilets anymore with the extra income coming into the house and he had even saved enough to buy a 1965 Mustang to restore one part at a time. He flirted with Mellanie Henderson, a tall brown-skinned girl who sat beside him in English class and wore sweaters as tight as her skirts were short. Between History and Geometry class they found a dark corner near his locker and when Alex closed his eyes and his mouth met hers, he didn't know the tongue was capable of doing such things. The world spun around him and he was caught in its whirlwind and didn't want to be set free. When she pulled away and adjusted her hair, he stumbled to class like a drunk man. At 17, one Friday night, he left his virginity on her living room couch when her parents were away.

But before Christmas break, everything his teachers were saying began to be drowned out by voices he'd never heard before. They kept telling him that he wasn't shit and wasn't ever going to be shit. Alex started talking back to them, telling them to shut up. But the voices became louder and more frequent and so he began to accommodate them. He accused Mom of poisoning his food, suspected Margaret of taking his money and cursed classmates whom he swore were talking behind his back. Mellanie too. He found all the van der Pool's he could on the internet and when he contacted them asked if any were his dad. For a week, after Mom had gone to work, he stayed in his bedroom staring blankly at the news channels. And when the TV wasn't on, he laughed remotely at its black screen. He heard George W. Bush in the walls and by the time he'd torn a hole in the paneling, Bush had escaped. He ran barefoot, shirtless down to Stovall High, burst into a Math class and declared that he was going to join Al Qaeda in high definition on CNN. He and his family would soon know the meaning of schizophrenia.

After two months of counseling, medications, and electroconvulsive therapy at Lakeview, it was mid-March and too late to return to Stovall High. He earned a GED by June and went on a two-month job hunt. When his phone never rang for a second interview, Alex enrolled in Stovall State that September. Of the thirteen hours he took that semester, all he remembered was his 9:30 poetry workshop with Dr. Bobby Hamilton. The first week Dr. Hamilton and his students excoriated him for his cultural references and mocked his style and technique. By the second week, his poetry was the punch line of their perverse sense of humor. As he gathered up his book bag, their mockery propelled him through the door and out of the school. Their laughter still echoed after all these years. In October, his cousin Raymond called from Memphis to wish him a happy 18th birthday, informed him that mid-South Distributors were hiring and that a change of scenery may do him good. His mother agreed and two weeks later, she moved with Alex to keep an eye on her son. Two days afterward, Alex was living and working in Memphis Tennessee.

Alex looked around the room once again, glanced at the ceiling. He couldn't believe after seven years, he was back where he started. He couldn't fully explain what happened or how it went wrong. All he knew was that the walls of his sister's house were closing in upon him and that he was stuck in Stovall.

And now the voices were back.

This time it was Tobi.

The house creaked under its own weight. Alex leaped from the bed as if it were on fire and when he did, the copy of *Native Son* thudded against the floor.

"Tobi? Tobi? That you?"

"Yeah, man. You expecting somebody else?" Tobi's laughter echoed throughout Alex's head, died in a remote corner of his mind.

"Kind of cold this morning." Alex brushed his hair by running his fingers through it. He rose from the bed, flung open the curtains and stood beneath a stream of soft morning light. He scratched his testicles through blue boxer shorts.

"Cold? Man, you need to wake up on the south side of Chicago in the dead of winter like I did one time. It was so cold I thought my balls was gonna turn purple and fall off. Where I was staying, I spent most of my time between fighting that hawk and side-stepping rats. You ever killed a rodent, van der Pool?"

He didn't give Alex opportunity to answer.

"I ain't talking 'bout no mouse with no trap," Tobi continued. *"I'm talking a rat the size of your head with teeth as long as your arm and sharp enough to take your leg off with one bite. If you don't have a lead pipe or a baseball bat handy, you'll be walking with a limp for the rest of your life. Feel like I been killing rats all my life."*

Outside, three bluebirds lighted upon a tree and

flew away. Their wings beat music upon the air, shadows across Alex's face.

"You ever kill anything, van der Pool?"

Alex sighed. The question reminded him of what day it was, that he was supposed to be in court at nine o'clock. "Naw. They said I tried to, though."

"Who is they?"

Alex turned around expecting to see somebody, but no one was there. He walked over to the dresser, inspected himself in profile, and stared at the white bandage over his right eye. "The Shelby County Criminal Justice System. DA tried to stick me with attempted second degree, but my lawyer got it down to a lesser charge."

"Lesser charge? Man, they done sent niggers to the electric chair on some lesser chargers. What happened?"

Alex shook his head.

"What?"

"I don't know."

"You better find out. You need a good lawyer? Look up Colin A Pride, Attorney at Law. He told me one time: 'Tobi. You stay out the cemetery, I'll keep you out of the pen' . . . Say, that DA's name ain't Wardell is it?"

"I don't know."

"What happened, van der Pool?"

Alex whipped around. "I don't know!" His words were fists punching the wall. He stumbled over a copy of *A Good Man is Hard to Find*, then regained his balance and stood over the bed. A clock on the bedside table intruded upon his thoughts. Its red face glared 8:30. In an hour his parents would be here to take him to his court appointment at noon in Memphis. "I don't know what happened and I don't care. All I know is I finally know what I need to do with my life"

Alex waited for the voice in his head as time ballooned, began to float away. He heard nothing this time. He waved his arm over the length of the bed, its sweep encompassing the contents that lay upon it. "Poetry," Alex said out loud, smiled wide and bright. He gathered a legal pad and a handful of loose sheets of paper and held them over his head. "I want to write poetry."

"Poetry? I don't know if I even know what that is. I couldn't afford to mess with no poetry."

"I can't afford not to." Alex rearranged several of the loose sheets of paper in his hand, shuffled them as though they were a deck of cards. "This is the only thing that's kept me alive the last two months, Tobi. Writing these poems, reading all these damn books. When I write, I'm not so agitated; things are clearer and relate to other things clearer. When I write, I know where I've been and why I went there and how I got to this point. Now, if poetry can do that, who needs Seroquel? Poetry is just like having wings on my back, man."

"You can't fly with fiction? I could get into a good novel."

Alex shook his head. "Ain't got time for a novel, Tobi. Things are moving too fast, seems like the days are all out of order now. All I have is this moment and poetry is like sticking your finger in an electrical socket. I'm on fire. I can do anything. I just want the world to know I'm alive."

"Hope you have a better trip than I did."

"Check this out, Tobi." Alex turned a sheet of paper right side up and began to read:

O' great night, God of creation, sun of the
moon
Why are you daylight upon me down at the peak
of shining?

You look faint back so weak at me O' great
moon and ever so
I tip my place it feels to be out to you for I know
how of hat.
But O' great temporary, these feelings are your
place only moon, for you'll find
As I'll find my Creator for we are committed
were made by the place and we
To him, his face thus be strengthened we are
glory destined to see and by his.
O' great forever you will be moon in that moment of strong you
And give night and day and your ultimate light
and it shall be done
When I'm made before His holy sight whole.

"Well?. . .Don't laugh at me, Tobi. That's the
worst thing you can do to a person. I've been laughed
at before about my poetry. That's not going to happen
again."

*"I ain't laughing, man. I don't know if it's good or bad.
Who gets to judge?"*

Alex nodded. "I'm going to find out if it's good
or bad. That's why I'm going to Stovall State. Today. I got *all* my papers in order this time." He held
up a handful of his poems for no one in particular.
"Ain't nobody or no thing going stop me from taking that poetry class either. I want to see what Dr.
Bobby Hamilton," he pronounced the name if it he'd
swallowed a spoonful of Castor oil, "has to say this
time."

Tobi cleared his throat. *"You sure you want to fool
around with that school?"*

"Poetry is life or death now. It's for real and its
forever. I should've done this several years back, but I

ran away from my calling. There's nowhere else to run now, Tobi. It's the only thing that matters."

"If you feel this way about poetry, why you been talking to me for the last month? Why not Shakespeare or some goddam body?"

Alex sat on the bed, dropped the papers beside him and laughed long and hard. When he finished, he lay back on the bed with his hands clasped behind his head. He was silent several minutes. "You changed everything, Tobi. You've given me the confidence to be whoever I want to be, to do whatever I want to do. Every day I wake up, I know you're going to be here to lead and guide me. All I got is you and all these books. For the first time, I was able to open a book, doesn't matter if its poetry or fiction and define myself, take a good look at the way I am. Until then I thought no one understood me, that I was the only one feeling this way. There are others out there, hundreds of us. I tried to talk to some poets. But they were too busy trying to get paid for poetry readings. Besides, you the only one that ain't never cursed me out."

"Not yet. Besides, I'm not who you think I am."

"What are you talking about? Who are you?"

"I'm Tobi. I'm just a voice in your head and if I'm in your head, that means that I really don't exist unless you allow me to then it's your own voice you are listening to anyway. Look man," Alex heard Tobi sigh, *"You can't live your life the way I do or the way anyone else has. Don't blame me if you screw it up and don't give me no credit if you get it right. I got enough problems. You and you alone got to decide who you want to be."*

"I am Tobi."

"I'll be damn. It's like that, huh? How old are you, van der Pool?"

"Twenty-five."

"You sure you want to go down to that damn college and take a poetry class? Have you forgotten what happened last time? You know these white folk don't want you doing nothing like that. If you don't do nothing else, you can always stay here. At least you getting plenty to eat and ain't sharing a room with four or five folk. I almost had a room of my own, once."

Alex sprang from the bed, stepped on a copy of *One Hundred Years of Solitude.* "And do the fuck what? Whether I go or don't go to that college, the only thing I have to lose is my life." He grabbed a book bag from the floor and stuffed it with poems, tossed it into a chair before walking into an adjacent bathroom.

After he showered, Alex grabbed a pair of scissors, chopped handfuls of his hair and dragged a razor across what remained until it piled around his feet. He massaged his scalp with lotion until it gleamed like a temple dome on the side of a mountain under a golden sun. Finally, he shaved his beard, meticulously trimmed his moustache, splashed cologne upon his face and applied deodorant underarm. He ripped off the bandage and revealed a wound with stitches over his right eye. He measured his new look in the mirror, nodded his approval, tossed the bandage and hair trimming in a waste basket, then exited the bathroom.

Upon re-entering the bedroom, Alex slipped on a book, stooped to grab it and held it up to the light. *The Collected Poems of Elizabeth Bishop.* The fish. The fish. She let the fish go! Alex loved that poem and would always laugh aloud when he remembered it. He removed underwear, a white pullover shirt and black pants from a dresser drawer, slipped into them.

"Tobi?"

He rambled a top drawer in a quest for a fresh pair of socks and when there were none extracted a .38 from beneath a stack of t-shirts. He released the cylinder to ensure that six bullets were in place, then zipped the weapon in his book bag.

"That's a good move, van der Pool. Everybody else walking round with one. But why you need to take one to college?"

"No, I haven't forgotten about what happened last time when I tried to get in that poetry class over at that college. Far as I got was the administration building. They said I didn't have all my papers in order and that I needed to come back when I did and when I tried to show them my poetry they said I was acting strange and called the law on me. That Sheriff." Alex fingered the scar above his right eye. "That goddam Sheriff throwing me on the concrete and hitting me with his nightstick for no reason. I hope like hell I run into that sonofabitch again. Yes. I remember what happened, Tobi. And so do you. But that was two weeks ago. They put me out that time. Ain't going to be no putting out this time."

"That kind of looks like the gun I used to have. Can I see it?"

"You've already seen it."

"You got a knife?"

Alex pulled the laces of his brown shoes into a tight bow. He wasn't wearing socks when he stood to his feet. "What I need a knife for?"

"You might run out of bullets. Besides, look like cutting a motherfucker's head off is the going thing nowadays."

Alex grabbed his book bag, swung it over his shoulder, had his hand on the doorknob, then remembered what he'd forgotten. Allowing the book bag to slide to the floor, he grabbed a legal pad and pen from the bed and standing with one foot on Emily Dickenson and the other on Walt Whitman, executed a flurry of writing across the page. He signed his name, tore the paper from the pad and folded it. He wrote Margaret's name on the outside of the paper and left it on the dresser.

He scooped up the book bag, opened the door and walked down the hall.

"Alex. Mama will be here in about thirty minutes. You ready?"

Alex ignored his sister's inquiry from behind her closed bedroom door. He made his way to the kitchen, flipped on the light, poured himself orange juice and set the empty glass in the sink. He slid open a drawer of forks and spoons, removed a butcher knife instead and zipped in it his book bag along with the pistol. He walked back towards his sister's bedroom, stood outside its door.

"Alex?"

"Yeah, Sis. I'm ready. I'm just going to step outside and get some air, ok? He paused, anticipated her saying something and when she didn't, he added: "I love you, Margaret."

There was silence from the other side of the door. "Outside? Alex. Don't go too far. They'll be here shortly. Is everything ok?" she stammered. "You all right? Alex?"

Alex opened the front door, paused on the threshold and looked back over his shoulder. "Tobi. This is it. You ready?"

"I'll see you down the road, van der Pool."

Alex closed the door behind him, crunched the crisp morning underfoot.

Warren Johnsey loaded the back of the pickup with the last of his fishing gear. He wanted to laugh aloud, but instead hummed a tune with no name, then entered his vehicle and put it in reverse. It was the first day of vacation, his last vacation and as he drove towards the river, he felt like a man who held the deed to the entire planet in his back pocket. He adjusted his baseball cap to fit loosely upon the back of his head. For the past 30 years, he'd been the sheriff of Moore County, which seemed more like a hundred years ago now. But it didn't matter, now. A year ago, he and his wife, Cathy, had buried their only son, David. And come November, just two months from now, he would bury this job too. He didn't know what he and Cathy would do; they would have to figure it out as they went along, but in sixty days, he was calling it quits. No more re-election campaigns, budget meetings, suits and ties, training seminars, assholes on the county commission. But he was calling it quits on his own terms. They, mainly the county commissioners, had tried to get rid of him for years. Said he was a 20th-century sheriff in a 21st-century world, the ghost of Bull Connor, last of the good old boys, a relic for a museum. They'd even set traps for him; he knew who they were. Misappropriation of government funds; that didn't work. Bribery, that didn't stick. And sexual harassment; he didn't even know what that was; hell, not so long ago a woman didn't mind being pinched on the ass in the office. He figured at one time or another all his enemies had taken their shots and had fired blanks or totally missed the mark.

And that's one thing he'd learned early, to know his friends from his enemies. Sometimes it was difficult to tell who your friends were, he thought; everyone smiles in your face when they want favors. But he always knew his friends. They were the ones who he'd grew up with as a kid, attended church picnics, Friday night ball games, married and struggled to raise families on factory pay. On election day, it was his friends who always punched the ballot beside his name every four years for the past three decades.

Sitting at a red light, Sheriff Johnsey reflected upon the changes he'd seen over the past two decades as the highest law enforcement official in the county. Typewriters had gone the way of dinosaurs. Everything was hooked up to some computer somewhere even when it wasn't hooked up. Revolvers were like slingshots compared to some of the firepower criminals were packing nowadays; he traded his .357 Magnum for a .40 semiautomatic seven years ago. And he thought he'd never see the day when he'd miss marijuana. If Sheriff Johnsey had his druthers, he'd take marijuana any day of the week instead of crystal meth. At least once a week, he and his deputies were busting up a meth lab somewhere and every time they busted one up, two more were found not far from where they busted up the first one, if the damn thing didn't explode and kill everyone involved first. And now the assholes were desperate enough to make it in their vehicles or on the side of the road. He shook his head.

But it just wasn't his county. Methamphetamine had become a commodity in west Tennessee like cotton, corn or soybeans. It was like a punishment from God eating up money, resources and the minds of those stupid enough to curse themselves with it. After twenty years on the job he could tell the criminal by the drug: if it was crack, nine out ten times niggers were involved; but white folks love crystal meth.

Sheriff Johnsey didn't know how long the light had been green and smiled sheepishly into his rearview mirror at an impatient motorist. He eased off the brake, accelerated, checked his watch but didn't really have to. His stomach told him what time it was. Every weekday morning, just before nine, he got the day started right with breakfast at the Downtowner Café. All the fellows would be there awaiting his arrival, a cross-section of the community: Marvin Bradbury, owner of Best Value Hardware Store; Tim Swinford, insurance agent; Johnnie Gardner, director of Gardner Funeral Home and Eddie Reed, retiree and people watcher from the courthouse square. And of course, Opal Mathis, who'd been a waitress at the Downtowner for as long as there'd been a Downtowner and knew how the Sheriff liked his country ham and eggs over easy, wheat toast and coffee black, no cream or sugar and never filed a lawsuit when he pinched her ass.

"What you say 'bout it, gentlemen?" called Sheriff Johnsey, approaching the table of four, taking his seat and removing his cap.

He watched them look around the restaurant, at each other as if not quite sure who was being addressed. "Don't insult us like that, Johnsey," replied Eddie Reed, slurping into his coffee.

"My apologies. You sons of bitches."

Tim Swinford pounded his fist on the table. "Now that's what I'm talkin' about."

"You working undercover today, Sheriff?" asked Johnnie Gardner, commenting upon the Sheriff's clothes of blues jeans, red flannel shirt, ball cap, sneakers. It always seemed strange not to see Sheriff Johnsey in a jacket and tie. He preferred plaids and stripes regardless of their coordination to one another or the retro fashion statement implied. A river of baldness flowed down the center of his head, leaving tufts of gray hair sprouting on both sides of its banks. His eyes, set within a clean-shaven face, were sharp and keen like gray lasers detecting and penetrating whatever came across his field of vision. On his right forearm was a souvenir of his stint in the Navy during World War Two, nights of drinking and dares in whorehouses and tattoo parlors; he considered it an honor to display an anchor with the battleship's name beneath it.

Sheriff Johnsey folded his arms and leaned on the table with a serious expression on his face. "Oh yeah. I'm working to apprehend a suspect. More than one as a matter of fact." His comrades shifted uneasily, eye-balled one another with half-smiles not really knowing when their long-time friend was serious or not.

"Is this a murder case, Sheriff?"

"Damn betcha." The expression on Sheriff John-sey's face began as a smile and ended as laughter that rose above all their heads. "And I'm the one doing the killing. I'm going to try and murder as many catfish as I can. Catfish, crappie, blue gills. Anything that's moving is in trouble." He checked his watch. "'Bout twenty minutes from now, somebody'll probably have to arrest me. I'll be a serial killing son of a gun."

All five men erupted, their laughter settling like confetti around their feet.

"You know what," Sheriff Johnsey listened to Tim Swinford begin his tale. Swinford, an ex-All State high school basketball performer, ran three miles a day, spent three days a week in the gym. At six foot six inches, he was tall even when he sat down. Dark brown hair, bushy eyebrows and a mustache, he wore a gold watch chain atop an immaculate three-piece blue suit, matching blue tie and Italian leather shoes. He was an agent for a major insurance company for eight years before starting his own agency seven years ago. "Speaking of fishing. When I was down in the Keys two summers ago, I was fishing with a doctor and a lawyer. Some big shots from Vermont of somewhere around there. So, we're all shooting the bull—"

"Yeah, you got plenty of ammo for that."

"Probably could've loaned 'em some."

"Anyway," continued the insurance salesman, "the lawyer had a yacht and were all out there drinking wine and deep sea fishing when the lawyer says 'You know. I had some rental property that got destroyed in a fire. That's how I bought this boat. With the insurance money.' The doctor said, 'that's interesting. I had some land got destroyed in a flood. That's how I end up buying a condo down here. Insurance money.' The lawyer got real quiet. Then after about ten minutes he asked the doctor, 'How the hell you start a flood?'"

The table swelled, rose and fell in waves of laughter. "Swinford," added Johnny Gardner, his tongue in his left cheek trying to remove a piece of bacon, "You ought to cut that stuff out, man." He became a mortician by osmosis, a third generation of Gardner's in the funeral home business. Started sweeping the floor when he was fifteen and practically grew up with the dead. While in college, he majored in music with designs of becoming the next Dave Brubeck and moved to Paris. Upon graduation, he shared a flat on the West Bank with three hippies—two guys and mademoiselle. Later, he would tell Johnsey about the good wine, how much hash he'd smoked and the intellectual psychobabble he'd engaged in during those times. He sat in with Art Blakey, Stan Getz, and even Dizzy Gillespie when they came to town.

But most of the time, he supplied rhythm in smoky jazz dens late into the early morning night. When a Parisian record company told he that he was too Avant Grade for the Avanti Grade, he cursed them out in broken French and slammed the door behind him. Gardner figured he was simply ahead of his time, his approach to composition being revolutionary and going against the status quo. And who needed the hassle, especially when you were broke and hungry and home a mere phone call away. Two days late and two years too long in the City of Light, when Dad met him at the airport in Memphis, he possessed nothing but a passport, the clothes on his back and his name.

"I tell you what," Gardner leaned forward, rested both elbows on the table, his nostrils flaring, "we had a funeral—and this is serious shit now—ten years ago, Sherry Davenport. You remember her, Sheriff? Married to Roger Davenport. Anyway, the funeral is over and everything and the pallbearers are leaving the church with the body and they accidentally bump a wall. And what in the hell you know?" Gardner looked from face to face around the table, paused adding tension before the climax. "Old Sherry ain't dead. Hitting that wall done something 'cause she goes to hollering and kicking and screaming to get out of that casket and hell you fellas know well as I do that she lived another 10 years after that."

"I thought you said this was serious shit?"

"It is. Seriously deep and wide."

"Sheriff don't remember no Sherry Davenport."

Gardner held both hands in the air. "Wait a minute, fellows. I'm telling you, she lived ten years after that. And when she did die, she really died this time. We had the body again and the service was in the same church and when it was over and the pallbearers were headed out the door to put the body in the hearse, her husband, old Roger Davenport yelled out: 'Hey, you sons of bitches. Look out for that goddam wall!'"

"Yeah, you gotta watch them women," Marvin Bradbury said. 'Specially these women today. Let me tell you what happen to me the other day." He was last of a dying breed. There were not many days when he didn't stop by the Sheriff's office to vent about keeping open the doors of an independent hardware store. What the hell for? When you had to compete against superstores like Lowe's and Home Depot with super inventories and super advertising budgets and super low prices, what the hell for? He was tempted more than once to follow everyone else and go shopping out there himself. Keeping an independent hardware store open in downtown Stovall, he almost convinced himself at times, was akin to opening a window and tossing his life savings out of it. But no matter how strong his own arguments were for slashing prices and putting up "going out of business" signs, being his own boss and the freedom it afforded always pushed him out of bed each morning. Besides, when your wife has preceded you in death by ten years and you don't fish or hunt there is only death on the other side of retirement. "Lady walks into the store and asks where the hinges are. I take her to where they are and she picks one out and examines it real close like she had something on her mind. So, being the dedicated service clerk that I am, I ask her if she wants a screw for that hinge. She says no—"

Marvin Bradbury halted his speech spotting Opal Mathis hoisting a plate of sausage and eggs with the Sheriff's name on it. She wore a white uniform beneath a pink apron, her blonde hair piled upon her head secured with several hairpins and she chewed gum as she made her way toward their table. She responded,

"You're welcome," and headed for a youngish couple just seated by the hostess.

Sheriff Johnsey marveled at her behind bouncing across the room, then rejoined with Marvin, Tim, Johnny like co-conspirators putting their heads together to discuss a matter of machination. "She says no. But I'll give you a blow job for that microwave on that shelf over there."

Marvin pounded the table, Tim stomped the floor, Johnny slapped thighs and the Sheriff grabbed his side to prevent it from cracking.

"Where she at now?"

"You get her phone number?"

"Which one of yall's wife was that?"

Their laughter blistered the morning air. Sheriff Johnsey knew this eatery like he knew every back road deep in the county. The Downtowner Café had moved from East LaGrange to McCaully Street in downtown Stovall. A mural of Percy Roberts, a country singer who frequented the Grand Old Opry and had a handful of Top 10 hits in his heyday of the Sixties, donned the side of the building. As Stovall's eternal native son, he was one of the town's few claims to fame. The restaurant's owners had added ceiling fans and hung antiques, anything from farm instruments to photos of persons unknown, upon the walls, adding a rustic ambiance to country cuisine. Checkerboards on all the tables served as a diversion between orders placed and food delivered. The breakfast and lunch crowds kept the bills paid, books in the black. But Stovall rolled up its sidewalks shortly after dusk and supper had never been a feasible option for the cafe.

"That reminds me of the other day," began Eddie Reed after a long gulp of coffee, "and I'm sitting on the courthouse square, me and Lacy Rhodes and Jimmie Perry with a German Shepherd beside my chair and we're discussing how to bring down the price of a barrel of oil and how to disarm North Korea and a whole lot of more shit when–"

"Did the dog have any ideas on how to save social security?"

"Hell, he was the smartest one in the bunch."

"The only one that could read and write anyway."

The only life Eddie Reed had ever known had been that of mules, plows, and overalls. His DNA was comprised of soybeans and cotton. Sheriff Johnsey had played baseball in the cow patches of Eddie's family farm as a youngster with Eddie and his brothers. There wasn't much Eddie couldn't tell you about farming. Once upon a time, he'd also tell you in this county a man could make a living with just a few acres of soybeans and cotton. And a few livestock to boot. But those days had long since passed along with the family farm swallowed by the competition of conglomerates, debt, and foreclosure. He was the lone survivor of the Reed clan living off Social Security benefits in a high-rise for senior citizens just across from courthouse square, days basking on courthouse benches beneath shaded sycamore trees, counting passersby on downtown streets, finding solace against the night with re-runs on cable TV and fifths of Jack Daniels. He was rarely without his St. Louis Cardinal baseball cap pulled low over his eyes, blue overalls, and black shoes.

"Anyway," Eddie Reed took up where he left off. "Fellow in a suit and tie, some damn Yankee, speaking of lawyers, walks up and asks me, 'Mister, does your dog bite?' I told'im, naw and kept on talking to Rhodes. Fellow reached down and tried to pet the dog on the head and what in hell he want to do that for? Dog damn near snapped off two fingers and half of another one and the New York fellow starts to hoopin' and hollerin and cussin' and jumpin' 'round before he asked me, 'Mister. I thought you said your dog don't bite!" I looked at 'im and shook my head and told 'im: That ain't my dog."

Sheriff Johnsey glanced out of the plate glass window and caught a reflection of Eddie pulling up the straps of his overalls, leaning back in his chair, his mouth greasy with a self-satiated smile, laughing louder and longer than anyone of the group. He told the same joke at least once a week and the other fellows' laughter was canned and on cue. Sheriff Johnsey figured that Eddie's dementia was no longer early stage and that it wouldn't be long before there'd be an empty spot at the table they shared together. So, no matter how many times he heard the same old joke, Sheriff Johnsey knew that laughing with Eddie was the right thing to do.

"Eddie, you getting a little too much sun out there," someone commented between laughs.

"You need to quit siccing dogs on folks, man. Fellow wasn't no civil rights worker was he?" guffawed another.

"Civil rights worker? Goddam. I remember when we used to ride through the streets of east Stovall late at night and pick up the first nigger we'd see. We'd take them out to McCauley's clearing and have all kinda fun with 'em. Sometimes they made it back, sometimes they didn't. I miss them days when everybody knew where the lines were drawn. Now, some of these niggers look at you like they dare you to say something to 'em and when you do, they'll get smart as hell with you." The tone of the conversation changed the atmosphere around the table the way a sunset changes the landscape falling behind the earth. Their faces aged and hardened with reminiscence.

Sheriff Johnsey finished the last of his sausage and

eggs, wiped his mouth with a paper thin napkin, belched beneath his breath. "Well, they ain't but so smart," he motioned Opal Mathis for a refill on coffee, black no sugar. "Woman got her purse snatched outside Food King on Tuesday. Nigger makes his getaway on foot and I catch up with him about 30 minutes later on Windmere Road, still running. I pat 'im, cuff him, read him his rights . . . and let me give you a friendly tip by the way. Anytime you see a nigger running down a road with no shirt on, whether he's got a pocket book or not, nine out of ten times he's either running away from a crime or running to commit one." Everyone giggled but the Sheriff. "Anyway, I got the suspect in the back of the car and I tell him, I'm gonna take him back to the scene of the crime for a positive ID. We roll back up at the Food King where the victim is still talking to some other officers and when I yank the suspect out of the car, and without saying a word to him—true story now--he takes a look at the victim and shouts, 'Yeah, Sheriff. That's the woman's pocketbook I snatched 'bout an hour ago!' I just looked at 'im and told 'im get back in the car, son."

The mood brightened as if the quartet were a terminally ill patient receiving news that his or her malady was now in remission. "Alright, fellows," Sheriff Johnsey concluded, blowing on his hot freshly poured cup of java, swallowing, "I got to get on down the road. See you next time. And don't let me have to bust none of yall's ass before then." Sheriff doffed his cap, left his fare and a tip upon the table, smiled and waved everyone so long.

"Take it easy, Esse."
"Holla at you later, homie."
"Peace out, my nigger."

3

Alex watched the Tennessee morning unfold. It was the fall of the year and the world looked as though it were one minute old. The crispness of the day, the colors in the landscape and the blueness of sky reminded him of a dream. And maybe today was all a dream. He hadn't been out of doors in two weeks and it was good to feel the sun upon his face and arms, the wind naked against his skin. He felt as though he'd dropped in on a familiar place after being away for a long time and things looked the same and didn't look the same. It was a good day for a long walk and Stovall State was at least ten miles away. Alex walked as though his senses were attached to an antenna, making him keenly aware of everything.

He readjusted the book bag over his shoulder and walked even faster. He reassured himself that as long as he was at the school by noon, everything was cool. Country living, he mumbled, was compatible with solitude, but it was hell as far as getting around, especially when you didn't have a car. Margaret would've let him borrow hers. That was cool too. She'd done enough. It was time for him to be his own man.

The longer he strode down the country road the stronger he felt his body become. He soon came to understand that ten miles in city were probably equivalent to twenty in the country, but it wouldn't matter if it were a forty-five-mile hike; he was determined to get where he was going. The morning wore a coat of many colors: verdant grasses, maples, oaks, dogwoods all ablaze upon the canvas of earth. White clouds drifted across cerulean skies. A cow lowed from a nearby farm. He inhaled, filled his lungs with autumn, released it, thought about the Miles Davis solo he'd fallen asleep to the night before. Miles' muted melody melting in his mind.

In the distance, he heard the faint whine of machinery harvesting fields ripe with the fruit of the season. He strolled past corn stalks that towered golden above his head; sauntered by fields satiated with soft, silky rows of cotton; ambled past the denseness of collards, mustard and turnip greens and Alex saw a couple of marijuana plants interspersed between the rows.

He skipped a small ditch to a neighbor's front yard and came face to face with a tree, its branches hanging low with purple, succulent plums, still wet from morning dew. Alex reached, plucked, devoured a morsel, its juices drooling down the side of his mouth; he spat the seed at his feet and grabbed a handful more, noticing the movement of curtains from an upstairs window, before leaping over the ditch and back down the road.

One by one, Alex threw back his head and popped a morsel of summer into his mouth, sucking the meat from its core and discarding the pit. He heard a rustling in the bushes and hoped it might be a mongrel mutt; he stopped, tensed, thinking it could be something even worse. Just as quickly the noise became silence as if tracking him.

"That you, Tobi? Tobi?"

"Yeah, van der Pool. It's me. When I said I'd see you down the road, I didn't mean it like this." Alex listened as Tobi's laughter rolled over the fields, faded against the horizon. He shifted his book bag, resumed the long walk toward Stovall State.

"But you know what," Tobi continued, *"this ain't half bad. In Chicago, all we got is brick and glass and steel and concrete. After a while, you start feeling like you made out of steel and concrete. Lot of damn noise from a lot of damn people trying to make a life out of all that concrete and steel. Sometimes that shit gets hard, man, especially when you're hungry with holes in your shoes and they still expect you to run the race. In Chicago, it's hard to breathe sometimes, let alone think. I didn't. I just acted. But down here, things don't seem so hard. Life just moves along whenever its wants to, kind of happens right before your eyes. Hell, if I was raised down here, I might have turned out a lot different."*

It was Alex's turn to laugh. "Man, you got to be kiddin' me! You're the penultimate bad nigger as far as I'm concerned. It wouldn't have made no difference where you was raised. If you was raised down south, it would've been just a matter of time before you would have killed one of these crackers. Maybe more than one. And instead of the electric chair, it would be the end of a rope. So, it really wouldn't have mattered. They would've got you sooner or later."

"Penultimate?"

"Yeah. I read that in Baldwin's book. That means you're next to the last. Don't get no badder than that," Alex smiled.

"I didn't know I'd been nominated. Shit. You ain't met the last bad nigger yet."

Alex tossed the remaining plums on the side of the road, began walking like a man with places to go and a short time to get there. About forty feet away on the left side of the road he saw a young woman descending front porch steps. She had to be in her early twenties in blue jeans and t-shirt, long black hair halfway down her back, a bronze skinned goddess with a designer purse draped over her forearm, car keys in hand. Here she was right down the road from him, Alex grimaced, and he didn't even know it. He could've kicked himself, but instead smiled and made his way over.

"Be careful, van der Pool."

Alex approached her. "Good morning."

The house was white framed with white pillars and blue shutters, adorned with an assortment of flowers and shrubbery lining the walkway that led to the entrance. The porch had a wooden swing suspended from two chains and looked especially made for indolent afternoons, the cool of summer evenings.

She tensed, used distance as a safe zone, fingered her key chain until all she had to do was aim and squirt Mace into his eyes if need be. "Yes?" With the back of her hand, she brushed back a lock of hair from her eyes and sized Alex up with a squint of vision.

"My name's Alex." He waited like a fill-in-the-blank question on an exam; she being the only answer to anything he ever wanted to know.

"Van der Pool. You need to work on your pickup lines. Maybe they got a class over at the college for that."

"Yes?"

He kept a respectable distance from her, relaxed his hands by his side, hoped his body language would put her at ease.

"Yes? She asked. "Are you lost?"

"Shit. The whole world is lost."

"No. I'm where I'm supposed to be." He saw that she focused on the wound over his right eye.

Alex wanted to laugh but shook his head instead. "Actually, I'm found. I'm Margaret van der Pool's brother . . . just right down the road a bit." He pointed towards the distance he'd traveled.

"Oh, you're Alex!" She relaxed, as color was added to her voice. Alex marveled at the way her breasts, neither big nor small, moved as she approached him with an outstretched hand. She had sparkling brown eyes in a pretty face, a smallish waist and Alex didn't have to look behind her to tell that she had a nice ass. The girl was fine. "I'm Delilah. Delilah Jones."

Her hand was soft and warm like the throat of a bird when he took it in his, she holding on longer than expected. "You have got to be kidding."

"Man, you drooling out of the side of your ass."

"Why do I have to be kidding?" It was beautiful the way her lips looked after there weren't any more words to make them move.

"You're a little too late," Alex said gently pulling away and rubbing the top of his head creating a glare that was almost blinding. "If I'd known I was going to run into you, I'd kept my 'fro."

"Where in the world have you been?" She stood with hands on hips. "Margaret told me you were coming to stay with her last month, but I thought you never showed; I've only seen her coming and going. You've been there all this time? Did she ever mention me?" Delilah frowned, sized up his answer to come.

"Man, this chick is as phony as the day is long."

Alex shook his head. "Never did. But that's ok. Making up for lost time can be a lot of fun."

"Really?"

"Really." He felt the flutter of wings against his rib cage. She reminded him of Caroline. "So," he shifted the weight of the book bag, "what do you do you do around here?"

"Banking. Loan officer. But not today. I thought I'd used some vacation time on such a gorgeous day. Isn't it beautiful?" She surveyed the world around her, inhaled deeply, released it with a sigh. "So," she tilted her head at an angle, "what have you been doing since you've been here?"

"Writing."

"Writing what?"

"Poetry. I'm headed to class now. Stovall State."

"Oh. You're a dreamer."

"Sister. You don't know the half of it."

"You're walking all the way to Stovall State Community College? That's a ten-mile walk. Now who's kiddin' whom?"

"Goddam. Who says whom? That shit ain't even necessary."

Alex laughed. "I can handle it. It'll give me a chance to think some things out. Besides, I'm not alone."

Delilah surveyed the landscape, re-focused her sights on Alex. "Uh . . . ok. I'm not quite sure what that means . . . but since you're a dreamer, it's ok." She opened her purse, reached inside. "But anyway, I can give you a ride."

"That proves right there that everybody who works in a bank ain't smart."

Alex protested weakly. "I couldn't impose on you like that."

"I'm going right by the college to jump on the interstate. I have a date with a shopping mall in Nashville today." Delilah slid on a black pair of sunglasses. "It's no imposition at all. Besides," she motioned towards her vehicle, "we have to start making up for lost time sooner or later. It's a good day to drop the top. Don't you think?"

"OK," Alex said trailing her to sleek red convertible in the driveway. "If you insist."

"Van der Pool. I apologize, man. You meet a broad and five minutes later, she's chauffeuring you anywhere you want to go. She work at a bank. She must be driving a Mercedes or a Lexus.

Why don't you find a deserted road and slide those panties off."

"Oh," Delilah said. "I forgot my phone. I'll be right back." She skipped up the walkway, over the steps, across the porch, and into the house.

Alex jerked around, looked over his shoulder. "Tobi. Do me a favor. Shut the hell up this one time, will you? This girl ain't that kind of girl. She's Caroline, just a shade lighter. She's special. I can get it right this time."

"Special? They're special for scratching an itch nothing else can reach. But they're also special for making you do things you didn't know you were capable of doing. I never found nothing special about no woman. Who is Caroline and what was so special about her?"

Alex had the passenger's door open, one foot on the floorboard, the other on the concrete driveway. "I'll tell you about it. You riding with us?"

"Us? Last time I rode in a car with a couple, I sat in the front seat squeezed between the two of them. I was walking down State Street. They offered me a ride and didn't have to offer another one. Anyway, they pulled out a bottle of liquor and started drinking and slobbering all over each other. Next thing I know we're pulled over in an alley and they in the back seat pulling their clothes off one another and I didn't get no wine or pussy that night. They didn't even hear me when I slammed the door, turned my collar up and started back walking . . . I'll pass. If you don't get none, you can't blame me for cock blocking. Plus, it's so beautiful out here; think I'll look around some more. I've seen a cow, heard a rooster crow and I always wanted to ride a horse. So, I'll see you down the road, van der Pool."

"All right, Tobi. Later."

Alex threw his book bag on the floorboard before Delilah backed out of the driveway. The two of them sped through sun and shadow of two lane back roads, country ponds and crops in fields until asphalt thoroughfares and steel mountains came into focus, flowed into a cityscape. Sarah Vaughn crooned from the CD player.

She glanced sideways at him. "What happened to your eye?"

Alex touched the spot on his forehead. "Oh, that. Carelessness. I was helping Margaret move some boxes in the attic and one came down on me," he lied. "Couple stitches and I'm as good as I ever was."

"That looks like a nasty cut. Shouldn't you have a bandage over it or something? It'll be worse if it gets infected."

"I hadn't thought about that." He pulled down the visor, looked at himself in the mirror. "I'll take care of it when I get back to the house." He flipped the visor back up. "Thanks."

"How long have you been writing poetry?"

"Not long. Not long at all. But I've been writing every day, much as I can anyway."

"Have you published?"

"Working on it. That's the reason why I'm headed to Stovall State. Publication, a book deal, all that would be nice one day. And maybe getting paid would be a good thing; I damn sure could use the money. But all I want to do now is just get better. Somebody over there at the college should be able to help." They passed Morgan's Grocery. Alex looked back over his shoulder at the store he used to ride his bike to for chips and soda when he was a kid; it had become a boarded-up, childhood memory. "So, how long have you been making all that money?"

Delilah's laugh rose warm and bright when she tilted her head back, opened her mouth. Her perfume, along with the speed of the car, made him dizzy.

"I've been at the bank since I graduated college six

years ago. Started out as a teller and been promoted every year. I'm not rich, but I'm doing all right, I guess. I do have my eye on a vice-president position one day, though." She flipped on her turn signal, entered onto the by-pass that encompassed the city.

Alex glanced at the clock. He was ahead of schedule. "Why can't you be the president?"

"Around here?" Delilah's query came with a furrowed brow. "I wasn't raised around here like you, but it didn't take me long to figure out the culture. They're simply not having that around here. Never have, don't think they ever will. So, I'm not ruling out being a bank president. I'm just ruling out being one in Stovall."

Smart. Fine. Pretty. Intelligent. Alex felt as though he was caught up in a whirlwind of something magnificent and mysterious. He always thought love was something you had to grow into, the way he did with Caroline. But at this very moment, he wanted to give all of his dreams, his life to Delilah. "I understand. That's why I got outta here right after high school. Sometimes I think the future forgot about Stovall or didn't know it ever existed. Anyway . . . so how much longer you gonna stick around?"

"I don't know. Long enough to get a little more experience. Why you ask?" She came to a four-way stop, yielded the right-of-way to a green pick-up.

Alex turned half-way in his seat to look as far as he could into her eyes. "I'd like to spend some time with you before you make your escape."

"I don't know. Maybe, Alex." She met his gaze before returning hers back to the road.

"Hey. Maybe ain't no." Alex swallowed hard. He sighed his disappointment. "I should be back to the house around four and I'll get your number from Margaret. Can we start there?

Delilah licked her lips. "Hmmm . . . I don't know how late I'll get back and I have an early morning tomorrow. I may be able to squeeze in a phone conversation." Mischief sparkled in her eye. "Under one condition . . ."

"Speak on it."

". . . Read me some poetry?"

"I'll do better than that. I'll write you one."

Minutes later, upon the outskirts of town, apartment complexes, and strip malls dotted the terrain and Stovall State Community College lay in the heart of the eastern landscape. Delilah stopped in front of the administration building before Alex grabbed his bag from the floor, opened his door.

"Hey . . . thanks for the ride. Hope I didn't take you too far out of your way." Alex looked over both shoulders, surveyed parking lot for anyone with a badge and a gun. With no one in sight, he spat on the ground.

"No apologies necessary. Oh . . . what's your number?" Delilah removed her phone from her purse.

Alex closed the door behind him, bent down to speak to Delilah through the open window. "I don't have one right now. But it's all right. I'll see you later on, ok?"

Disappointment clouded Delilah's face, turned down the corners of her mouth. "Alright, Alex. Have a great day."

Margaret van der Pool greeted her mother and stepfather with hugs and kisses soon after she welcomed them into her home.

"Mama. We got to do something about Alex. He's not getting any better. As a matter of fact, he's only getting worst."

She placed their jackets and sweaters on racks and hung them in a hall closet. It was an hour and a half drive from Memphis to Stovall and Edna Madison and her husband Salvador preferred to stand and stretch upon entering. Edna vowed that after her first husband walked out on her, she didn't want anything to do with marriage again. Wasn't once enough for anyone? She'd managed all these years without a man. But after Salvador came along, she'd decided that it was one of the best decisions she could have ever made. Instead of both of them trying to shape and mold one another like young couples do, she accepted him for who he was and he did the same. They were married to themselves before they decided to become one flesh. She was 55 with a youthful figure, bright brown eyes, copper-skinned with a small mole on her left cheekbone. Edna wore her hair in a long black ponytail, had a bounce to her gait, each word of her speech enunciated with a breath of dignity. She was still a secretary, but this time for two Baptist churches in Memphis. Salvador, twelve years her senior, retired from the Steel factories of Gary, Ind., moved back south six years ago, met his bride a year later. Both vowed to make their marriage an eternal honeymoon, this being his second trip to the altar as well, with two grown kids married with kids of their own still up north. He was a couple of inches shorter than his wife, stockily built from 20 years of 12-hour shifts in the din of sweaty steel shops and had a receding hairline, graying around the edges. He preferred his shirt opened at the first three buttons, revealing a gold cross and a bush of black chest hair.

"I know baby," Edna Madison comforted her daughter by pulling her close to her, suspending the moment in a hug before releasing her at arm's length. "I've already talked to the judge. He's agreed to send your brother to the hospital. In a couple of hours, everything will be resolved."

Margaret's forehead wrinkled. "Judge Morris is going to send Alex to Lakeview? Instead of jail?"

"Yes."

"How'd you work that out, Mama?"

"Prayer. You and I and Salvador know good and well that my baby don't belong in no jail. And the good Lord knows it better than any of us. Now, I have put it in His hands and I'm through with it. So ain't no need in you holding onto it either. Just give God the glory. We sure don't deserve it." Her face became radiant as if looking at a great light only she could see.

Salvador came around his step-daughter, draped his arm around her shoulder. "Amen to that sister. Now, what time we gonna eat? I know you burned me some of them links and flapjacks, huh?"

At the breakfast table, Margaret added final touches to the setting with juice, coffee, water, napkins, and condiments. Fresh cut roses bloomed from the center of the table in a crystal vase, scenting the air with memories of summer. The languid September sun rested upon the room like light from an impressionistic painting. Mom, dad, daughter were seated around the table awaiting brother to complete the circle.

"Alex!"

"That boy don't eat enough to feed a bird. I don't see how he stays alive, Mama. He locks himself in that room, barely comes out for days, except when he went up to Stovall State a couple weeks ago. I still don't know what possessed him to do that. All I could get out of him was 'poetry.' But thank you again, Mama, for intervening and having him released to my custody. You're always able to work things out, somehow."

"The Good Lord worked that one out. After finding out about that incident with Caroline, they didn't want to. But no one got hurt this time and they finally took his diagnosis into consideration. God is good all the time."

"But I'm still worried. All his time is spent listening to jazz music and acting strange. I think he has read every book I've ever owned. And guess what he asked me the other day?" She didn't give her mother time nor reason to inquire. "'Why did we kill God?' He said that without even changing expressions. So I asked him who was 'we' and to leave me out of it and what made him think he was big and bad enough to kill God anyway?"

"What did he say to that?"

"Said 'what you mean leave you out of it? Whether you had anything to do with it or not, you still got to carry the body.' Then, just got up and went back into his room." Margaret shrugged her shoulders, lifted a cold glass of water to her lips, sipped. She styled her hair cropped close at the ears, had ebony eyes that penetrated perceptively and wore a loose flowing gown adorned in African mud cloth. With resolute steps, her slippers scraped and flopped as if to leave floors scarred.

Dad shifted in his chair, cleared his throat. "Well, you gotta consider that he hasn't been himself lately. Maybe the last three months or so. He's just going through a tough spot right now like we all do sooner or later. His is just a little tougher than most. But he'll bounce back. Once he gets back on his feet, he'll be ok."

Margaret exchanged her step-father's optimism for a wan smile and several nods of the head. She wanted to agree with his positive outlook on the future, but to do so would betray her own insincerity. The future to her was not six months spent in a mental institution or time in jail or prescription medication. She loved her baby brother and she needed some type of assurance that he would be all right if she wasn't around one day or if mom and dad wouldn't be there to throw lifelines every time he was going down. Staying with her for a couple weeks, months or maybe a year was fine. But it was going to come a time when he would have to stand and make it on his own. She couldn't keep beating up gang bangers. She had her own dreams to pursue, whims to chase and future to acquire. For Margaret, at 30, time was poised to slam the window shut on her opportunity for a husband and kids. Hell, she figured she'd never get married now. All her girlfriends were a testament to that. No man wanted to marry a Black woman over thirty years old. And what Black woman in her right mind wanted to have kids after thirty? Sometimes the future seemed a vague outline that had nothing to do with her life. Other times it was a tangible roadmap with detailed journeys and destinations. But right now, all she could see was temporary solutions to long-term problems and where was the future in all of that?

"Right now I'm starting to worry more about you than I am your brother," Mom placed her hand atop her daughter's, squeezed gently. "I've never seen you so much on edge before. Is it something else going on we should know about?"

"No." She wrapped her fingers around her mother's hand.

"Well, it's no point in you making yourself sick, worrying. I know you've been under a lot of stress dealing with Alex and we thank you for everything you've done in trying to help him out. You're a good sister and a wonderful daughter. But you can breathe now. Everything's been worked out."

Margaret released her mother's hand. "What in the world is that boy doing?" She pushed herself from the table and started down the hallway. "Alex!" When he didn't answer, she tapped lightly on the door, pushed it open and found the bedroom empty. She made her way back to her parents. "He's not here. He said he was going to get some air, but I thought he just stepped outside. I reminded him about the court date."

"I think by the time we finish eating, he should be back," Salvador said. "He couldn't gone too far, not out here in the boondocks anyway."

Edna shook her head, admonished her husband. "I need to get you to a doctor to get that hole in your stomach patched up." She turned her attention to Margaret. "This'll be a good time to count your plates and saucers. He may eat those too."

"C'mon baby. Don't be like that."

Margaret set the sausage, eggs, pancakes upon the table, grabbed a bottle of syrup, then sat down. With bowed heads, Salvador did the honors of beseeching God's blessings upon the food, the one that prepared it and the home in which it was to be served.

"So, how was the drive up, Dad?" Margaret reached for a toothpick, dislodged a strand of sausage from the gap in her front teeth.

"Oh, it was fine. Got love this time of the year. Before long I'll be in a tree stand, spying a buck. Nothing like deer tenderloin." Salvador wiped his mouth, dropped the napkin back on his lap. "Matter of fact, next time we come up I'll bring you some out of the freezer. Might throw in a rabbit too. Talk about good eatin'. I don't know if it gets any better than rabbit, gravy, and biscuits. Can't nobody burn a rabbit like your mama. You know how to cook 'im?" He smiled as if he'd just taken a bite of rabbit.

"Don't pay him no mind, Margaret," Edna added. "I hate cooking those things. Sometimes they still have buckshot in them. Anyway, how's life at the hospital?"

Margaret sipped her juice. "I guess the ER will always be the ER, especially on the weekend. Been thinking about transferring. You never know what will come through that emergency room. Weekend before last, one of my classmates, Mike Ryan, was in a car accident and we did everything we could and had him stabilized for an hour or so, but it wasn't enough. We go all the way back to sixth grade. Some things are harder to leave in the ER than others, but you don't have a choice."

"Well," Edna sighed, "maybe you need new faces, new scenery."

Margaret's face illuminated with a smile. "That's exactly what I was thinking. I have an interview at John Hopkins in a week."

"Where's that?" Salvador asked between swallows.

"It's in Baltimore"

Salvador almost choked on his coffee and when he cleared his throat, he and Edna exclaimed: "Baltimore."

Margaret enunciated her words with self-confidence. "Yes. Baltimore, Maryland. The job will be a promotion if I get it and the change of scenery will do me good. I have to give Alex credit. He left this place right out of high school to make it on his own and did all right by himself for awhile. Besides, there's nothing to keep me here anymore."

'Maybe so," Edna advised, "but don't ever feel like you have to run away from something that wasn't your fault. You didn't call off the wedding, Darius did. Maybe he should be the one to move to Baltimore. Or somewhere." She stabbed half a sausage with her fork, shoved it in her mouth. "You ever see him?"

"No. Only in passing. And that's close enough. My decision to move and nothing is set in stone yet, has nothing to do with anyone but me."

"Well, do me a favor," Edna requested. "Will you pray about it?"

Margaret batted her eyes to keep tears from spilling onto her cheeks. "Of course. You're my mother. Do I have a choice?"

"Amen to that," Salvador said. "Now, pass those eggs before they get cold."

Margaret and Edna looked at each other, shared laughter without sound.

"I don't know where that Alex is. The last thing he needs is to be late for court." Margaret finished her breakfast, dabbed the corners of her mouth, then dropped the napkin across her plate. "You know what he said to me a few minutes ago?"

Salvador checked his watch. "We're good. He'll show in a minute. What he say a few minutes ago?"

"He said 'he loved me.'"

"What's wrong with that?"

"Nothing. Except that he has never told me anything like that since we were kids. I tell you, that boy is acting really strange, Mama. Sometimes, I can stand outside his bedroom door and hear him talking to himself as though someone else is in the room with him."

"Could've slipped a girl in when you wasn't look-ing." Salvador winked. There wasn't a crumb on his plate as he drained his cup of coffee.

Margaret shook her head. "There's a girl down the road that I was going to introduce him to, but I could never get him out of his room. But it's too late now."

"You ever tell him that?" Edna pushed her plate away, propped her elbows on the table and rested her chin upon her hands.

"Tell him what, Mama?"

"That you love him?"

Silence settled upon the table, hushed everything that stirred the room.

"No. Can't say that I have."

"Well, it's never too late for something like that." Margaret felt her mother's hand gently squeezing her own.

"That was a quite a breakfast young lady." Salvador grabbed all the plates and silverware from the table and started towards the kitchen. "I ain't got no money, but I can always wash some dishes."

Alexander van der Pool wandered the Administration Building for an hour, became disoriented in a labyrinth of offices, hallways, and corners, then stopped a young brunette wearing a blue jean jacket, black slacks, brown shoes and piercings through both eyelids. When he inquired about poetry, she instructed him down the stairway at the end of the hall and to follow the walkway until he came to the last building on the right.

Ten minutes later, Alex stood on the sidewalk, his eyes scaling an ivy-covered building until they rested upon the raised letters of Dyer Hall. He looked over his left shoulder, heard a noise over his right.

"Tobi? That you? Tobi?

He squinted, saw that it was only debris scraping the pavement in a vortex of dance. He climbed a flight of steps, walked the long hallway. He passed bulletin boards congested with tutoring services, opportunities to travel abroad, auditions for *Othello*. Along the wall on the opposite side was a green and gold banner: Go Bobcats! Alex walked the length of the entire hallway twice, passed classrooms with closed doors, but none with poetry written on them. He came to an open office door with the name Dr. Howard Mayes on it and stood on its threshold.

"Excuse me." Alex shifted his weight from one foot to the other as if the floor were a bed of hot coals.

A blonde man in a blue cardigan, white shirt, and green tie sat at a desk typing furiously on a keyboard.

Three walls of his office bore the burden of books from floor to ceiling. He looked over the top of his black framed glasses, grimaced. "Yes."

"Could you tell me where Dr. Bobby Hamilton's class is?"

"Dr. Bobby Hamilton? Dr. Hamilton hasn't been here in four years." Dr. Mayes leaned back in his chair, its springs squeaking. He scrutinized Alex from his bald head to his brown shoes. "But the class is still around. It's not poetry. Just a literature class on the second floor. Megan Fly is the instructor." He corrected his posture, directed his attention back to his typing.

"Dr. Megan Fly?"

His printer lit up and blinked with a whined, expectorated paper. "Megan Fly. She's not a doctor, but she has an MFA. Who doesn't have one of those these days?" He laughed under his breath. "Room 223. You're about thirty minutes late." When Dr. Mayes turned around, Alex was gone.

Before Alex saw classroom 223, he knew he was in the right place. A female voice on the other side of the door had the words 'Harlem Renaissance' sailing into the hallway. Alex leaned his back against the concrete wall, closed his eyes and sighed. He imagined the professor standing before her class in black heels, a beige dress with a black belt and black trim around the neckline. She would be late forties, hair dark and closely cropped behind her ears. Alex visualized her standing before the class with her head slightly tilted and her mouth wide open, a book in one hand, pointing at nothing in particular with the other hand. He cocked his head at an angle to catch every word that slid beneath the door. What she said next made his heart beat faster.

"The Harlem Renaissance, originally known as The New Negro Movement, began in the early to mid-1920's and lasted until about the time the stock market crashed. Anyone remember 1929 from Dr. Mayes' history class? Well, what you should remember about the Harlem Renaissance is that it represented a time in American history when the arts—literature, painting, music—produced by African Americans was not only reborn, but thrived. This was a concerted effort by African Americans to assert their dignity, pride, and humanity through their art and by doing so taking on racism head on. A few of the key players during this movement were: Sterling Brown, Countee Cullen, Georgia Douglas Johnson, Nella Larson and visual artists Augusta Savage and Jacob Lawrence. But you can't talk about the Harlem Renaissance without mentioning the name of Langston Hughes."

Alex felt tears warm on his cheeks. He wiped them away, flung open the door and stumbled inside. "I wanna be a poet!"

The instructor resembled a statue in a city park on a cold winter's day, her students' faces frozen with fear, their mouths agape. Alex's voice was absorbed by the silence as if the walls were made of cotton. She looked exactly as he had envisioned her, except for the long silver earrings that dangled from her lobes and the diamond ring on her left hand. When the book she was holding slid from her hands and thumped against the floor, sound and motion returned to the classroom.

"Excuse me?"

"Are you Mrs. Fly?"

"Yes, I am." She picked the book up from the floor, set it on her desk. "And who are you barging into my classroom like this?"

"I'm Alexander van der Pool." Alex unzipped his book bag on a vacant desk on the front row, removed several pieces of paper and waved under Mrs. Fly's nose. "I wanna be a poet."

"Well, right now, the only thing you're doing is interrupting. Are you registered for this class?" She picked up a folder from the corner of her desk and perused it. "No. No, you're not."

The muscles in Alex's jaw twitched. "No. You don't understand. I've written these poems, been writing 'em for the last two months and I need to know if they're any good. You're the poetry teacher, right?

"Sir, I need you to go over to the Registrar's Office and sign up for this class. You're only a week behind. When you come back, you'll learn everything I know about poetry."

Some of the students snickered.

Mrs. Fly dropped the folder back onto the desk as if it were the last thing she would ever do for the rest of her life. Alex heard a door slam somewhere, its echo spread down the hallway; he flinched

"Tobi?" He looked over his shoulder towards the door. "Tobi? That you?"

"Yeah. It's me van der Pool. So you finally got what you wanted"

"I didn't think you were gonna make it."

"Man, I got here before you did. You didn't see that horse parked outside?"

Alex laughed out loud, almost doubled over. "Naw. I didn't see no horse."

"I didn't tie him up. Ain't no telling where he is by now."

"Mrs. Fly?" A red-haired kid with blood-shot eyes wearing a Muddy Waters t-shirt scratched his head and lifted his voice from the third row. "You need me to go for help?"

Mrs. Fly nodded her head once. "Would you please, Brandon?"

Alex, seeing Brandon turn sideways and push himself up from his desk, rushed to his book bag. "Hell, no." He laid his papers beside it, removed gun and knife from its compartment brandishing one in each hand above his head. "Ain't nobody going no goddam where and ain't nobody going for no security. I'll die before I go out like that again. Hell, everybody will die."

A collective gasp sucked the air from the room. Two blonde females bolted pass Alex out the door, left a shriek to haunt the room. Mrs. Fly covered her mouth, but couldn't stop a scream from slipping through her fingers. Brandon turned pale in preparation to faint, decided to sit back down instead before he did so.

"That's a bold move, van der Pool. How you feel?"

"Feels like it's my life now."

"See there. You brought me down here for nothing."

Alex corralled everyone to the back of the room, counted ten students plus Mrs. Fly. He ordered them to stand tables on end, barricades against what he could and could not see.

"Tobi? Tobi. We did it."

"We? Man, I ain't holding no gun or knife. I don't know nothing 'bout taking nobody hostage. But I will say this: it might be a good idea to close that damn door over there."

Alex tiptoed towards the door. Halfway there, he turned, pointed the gun at the hostages. "The first motherfucker that moves won't move again!" He pressed his back against the wall, peeped left and right into the hallway with the gun in one hand and seeing no one in sight, slammed the door shut with the hand holding the knife. He skipped to the back of the room, stood behind his hostages who stood behind barricades, everyone staring silently at the door before them.

"Alright," Alex breathed, leveling his gun at the door. "Let's see what now."

6

Sheriff Warren Johnsey sat on the banks of the Forked Deer River and thought that this must be his day. He couldn't believe he'd caught twenty catfish in less than an hour and a half. He figured with his luck, there was no need for baiting a hook anymore. Just cast the line in the water and reel 'em in. Or better still, simply open the cooler and the way things were going, they would jump right in. He figured he'd better stop at the convenience store on the way home and buy a few lottery tickets.

Sheriff Johnsey couldn't ask for anything more: the fish were hot, the beer was cold and it was a gorgeous day. Everything had a softness about it as if the cooler temperatures had rounded the edges off the long hot days of summer. The lake shimmered in ripples, murmured a tongue only known to itself. He looked overhead and couldn't find a cloud in the sky, only a bright sun reflecting itself in the twist and turns of the water. Somewhere, music escaped the throat of a bird.

This had become his favorite spot and time of the year. In the spring, he had to keep one eye on snakes basking under a new sun and in summer, he spent most of his time swatting ravenous mosquitoes. But the fall in the early part of the day was a sanctuary where he could remove his hat, pray and find peace in the essence of things. It was David's favorite spot as well. Sheriff Johnsey reached over and grabbed a bottle by the neck, drank his beer. Physically, he sat on the riverbank with his pole in hand watching for the float to disappear beneath the surface of the river, but mentally it was thirty years ago and David was by his side.

They had excavated worms the day before, secured them in a plastic bucket and early the next morning set out with fishing gear, soda pops, sandwiches and discovered this spot by the side of the river. He had rod and reel and David a bamboo pole almost as long as himself. Father taught son how to impale a three-inch writhing worm upon the end of a hook and when David stuck his finger with the pointed metal, Sheriff Johnsey didn't coddle or caress him, simply pulled out the first-aid kit and applied an antiseptic, stated: "You keep crying like that you gonna run all the fish off. Then what you gonna eat for supper?" David shook his hand, sucked his finger until the pain and blood subsided simultaneously before pulling his first fish from the muddy current: a five-inch Bream. Sheriff Johnsey stood back and watched David jump and scream with all the joy and happiness his seven-year-old body could contain and what it couldn't contain spill out of him and infected the Sheriff until he hooped and hollered and hopped just as far and wide as his son. That was a good day and there were other good days that followed in this self-same spot.

When David was 13, they laid their poles down about mid-day and Sheriff Johnsey led him into the woods. He set an old rusty can on a tree stump, removed a 9mm from his waistband and instructed David how to insert the clip, pull the slide, aim, shoot. David reminded him of himself at that age when he first shot a pistol, his mouth a line of concentration as he closed one eye, sighted the barrel of the gun and carefully squeezed the trigger. And just a year and a half ago after reeling in a red Buffalo fish, David now 33, told his father that he'd finally met the girl he wanted to marry.

Or thought so anyway.

"Boy, marriage is just like a three ring circus: first, comes the engagement ring, then wedding ring and then finally the suffer-ring . . . so go ahead and be unhappy like everybody else." Sheriff Johnsey laughed more at the prospect of having grandkids than at his own joke. He and Cathy tried to have more kids, but to give David a baby brother or sister failed numerous times. They had spoiled David and it was nothing either of them could do about it now and they'd promised that if they ever had grandkids, they would be spoiled rotten. Sheriff Johnsey became serious. "When'd you meet her?"

David was attaching a lure. "Couple weeks ago. She's quite remarkable, Dad. Her name is Rachel." He cast his line upon the waters, its arch a rainbow across the sky. "How'd you know you would marry Mom?"

Sheriff Johnsey took a long swallow from his beer. "Ah, you just know what you know, I reckon. But give it some time, son. How old is Rachel? Can she cook?"

"Twenty-seven. I don't know yet."

Hmmm. Two boys and a girl, Sheriff Johnsey thought. "How much time? It's hard to say. But I say go for it. Marriage is a good thing. Keeps you responsible and out of the streets and teaches you what it means to be loved and to love somebody, whether you like them or not." Sheriff Johnsey reeled in his line, recast it.

David took a swig from his beer. "Thanks, Dad. That makes me feel a whole lot better."

The short successive vibrations on Sheriff Johnsey's hip shook the foundation of his dream. He reached down, slid the cell phone from its case and recognized the office at once.

"Johnsey."

He heard a jet ski before he looked up and saw it as a blur down the river.

"What kind of incident?"

Sheriff Johnsey pushed himself up from the dirt.

"Is it a hoax?"

He swallowed hard, started gathering gear with his free hand to toss into the truck.

"I'm on the way."

7

Salvador dried his hands on a dishtowel, cut out the kitchen lights and joined his wife and step-daughter in the den. They were watching a Japanese man trying to guess the price of a box of spaghetti to win a trip to Australia.

"I don't know where he could be," Margaret sighed, getting up from her seat and leaving the TV to her parents. She stood on the front porch and looked both ways hoping to see her brother coming from either direction. Maybe she missed something the first time. After several minutes, she re-entered the house and walked towards his bedroom.

Edna looked at her watch on the underside of her wrist. "Well, it's a quarter after eleven. We're not going to make that court date and so they'll issue a warrant for him and pick him up." She looked at Salvador with doleful eyes. "Either way, we'll get him some help."

Salvador sucked a piece of meat from his teeth. "I was sure hoping to talk to Alex today. Had a proposition for him."

"Proposition? What kind of proposition?" Edna asked.

"That's between the two of us, baby." He winked at his wife, pulled a cell phone from his breast pocket. "Guess I better let his lawyer know." He punched speed dial, looked up at Edna. "I'll call the cops too, let them know he's off his meds so they'll know how to handle him."

A breaking news bulletin interrupted the game

show, a Hispanic woman giving a live report.

"Margaret?"

"It's me, Mama," she projected her voice throughout the house. "I didn't see him. I'm going to check his room this time."

"Something's happened over at the college."

Margaret came back into the room, stood to the side of the TV and watched the Hispanic woman with dark brown hair in a blue blazer report excitedly from the campus of Stovall State Community College. Margaret shook her head. "Why in the world would anyone want to do something like that at Stovall State?"

She didn't wait for an answer as she walked down the hallway into Alex's bedroom where she slipped and nearly fell from the volumes of books littering the floor. "Oh my God." She began to pick them up one by one, arrange them into some semblance of order until she was able to make her way to a window to raise it high. She scrutinized scribble on a sheet of loose-leaf paper:

> White man
> You have far too long and me
> For life my all
> I've boot lived heel under your too long
> With shackles toiled around my ankles, I
> Hot fields under day in your noon sun
> I listened tortured cries to the helplessly
> Of my night being violated in the heat of women.
> I've witnessed earth give forth a fertile God's
> Strange black hate dangling from your trees of
> fruit.
> I'm hurting your whips scarred from my mind
> And away ripped self-esteem.
> You've killed Malcom all Medgar my Martin:
> And forbid footsteps on God if the sun sets

In your neighborhood.
I can't should and why take anymore have t?
I am too a man
I am a man.
I am a man.
If I must strengthen God, demonstrate me.
If I must protect God protest me.
If I must forgive God kill me
White man
You have far too long and me
For life my all
I won't take anymore.
I refuse to.

It was unmistakably Alex's handwriting and she recognized the same penmanship on other pieces of paper, some with lines crossed through them, words written in the margins; those that he discarded were like tennis balls lying on a vacant court, none of which made much sense. She plucked balled up pieces of paper from the floor and was about to toss them into the trash when she noticed a medication bottle in the bottom of the wastebasket. "Oh my God." It was Alex's prescription for Seroquel and the bottle was full. Margaret was about to share the discovery with her mother and step-father when she saw her name lying at an angle across the dresser. She picked up the envelope, unfolded its contents:

Dear Sis:

Thank you for everything you've done for me for the past two months. I could never pay you back and I know you wouldn't let me even if I could. You have always been a great big sister and a good friend. But it is a good possibility that I am going to die today. Somebody is going to die because somebody is always dying. I am going to Stovall State today and I don't know if I'll ever see you again. I am taking with me my poetry, a knife, and a gun. Of the three poetry is the greatest of all. And will get answers for my life one way or the other. Don't worry. I am not alone. Tobi's got my back. Tell Mom and Salvador that I am sorry things had to go this way, but please know that I will always love you all.

Alex

Margaret opened her mouth and screamed, "Oh my God" as she ran through the house, the letter flailing in her hand.

6

"Alex? Alex?"

Alex heard the faint echo of his name travel through a great distance before it gathered strength, spread in waves against his ear. He blinked twice and Meagan Fly came into focus looking over her shoulder.

"Alex. We have a couple people here who need medical attention right away." Alex looked to his right saw a Black man in his late fifties with flecks of gray hair down on one knee holding his right hand to his chest. He wore a green pull-over with a white under-shirt beneath it and black slacks. He struggled to in-hale and exhale as if a concrete block were tied to each breath. Standing next to him was a white woman in her late thirties with pale skin who looked as though she would collapse at any moment into a pile of ashes.

"Alex. Mr. Wilson and Ms. Hudacek are in trouble."

Alex looked from Mrs. Fly to the two people in questioned. "All right." He followed them towards the door, watched them lean on each other and disappear through it. He put the knife back in his book bag and resumed his position behind his hostages.

"Man, how long we got to stand up like this? We been looking at that goddam door for an hour. My knee starting to hurt." The black teenager's afro was wide and deep enough for a bird to roost in it and he not even know it, more halo than a hairstyle. He was tall, slim, wore a goatee of whiskers braided beneath his chin and was centerfielder for the Stovall State baseball team where he batted left, threw right.

Alex leveled his gun at Monte's head.

"He's got a point, van der Pool. That door ain't going nowhere. But you might want to look out of this window."

Alex put just enough distance between himself and his captives to get off a shot in case someone tried anything stupid. He separated two slats of Venetian blinds with his index finger, and peered into the space between them. He squinted down upon a flurry of blue lights, yellow tape, the hum of news and law enforcement vehicles parked at jagged angles and bystanders clustered in small groups. There were cops in camouflage with assault weapons strapped on their backs. Alex panned right and his eyes rested on a white-haired man in a thick green vest talking to a white woman in a gray suit. When the woman walked away, Alex watched the white-haired man kick something on the ground, then look in the window he was looking out of. He removed his index finger, the blinds closing against everything that belonged to the world.

"All right. Everybody get down. " Alex ordered everyone against the back wall in a semi-circle. He sat lotus style on the floor in front of them, scratched his bald head with the butt of the gun. "All right."

7

Sheriff Johnsey arrived at Stovall State Community College an hour after he got back from fishing and was briefed on the situation. "Van der Pool?" The Sheriff frowned, tried to associate the name with memory. "Black boy?"

"Yes sir, Sheriff," answered a blond, pimply-faced deputy. "You arrested him yourself a little over two weeks ago for trespassing and disturbing the peace right here on this campus."

The Sheriff nodded. "Yeah. I remember. He's a couple bales of cotton shy of a wagon load. We released him to the care of his mother who convinced me that he wasn't dangerous. He staying with his sister out on Granger Road. I knew I should've sent his ass back to Memphis. Dammit."

As the chief law enforcement officer of the county, Sheriff Johnsey ordered the school to be shut down, the area evacuated and the SWAT team deployed. He donned a bulletproof vest, gathered his men around him and together reviewed floor plans of Dyer Hall. It wouldn't be a difficult assault, but he needed to know who he was dealing with and how to communicate with him. Right now, he had nothing to do but wait, wait for more background information on van der Pool, wait for the college President's Office to hand over a list of names of students, the teacher ,and their cell numbers so he could find out exactly what in the hell this guy wanted and why. Was this a disgruntled student, a terrorist, a madman? Or a combination of all three? So far, no shots had been fired and no one had been hurt. Matter of fact, two hostages escaped unharmed and the release of two other hostages was a good sign that this thing would be resolved quickly and they would not be here long at all. Over the years, he'd been involved in three standoffs and each was different from the last. But they were all domestic in nature. He convinced folks to come out with their hands up in one incident, tear gassed a suspect out of another and the final situation had ended in a murder-suicide. But this was different. This was an institution of higher learning and it was State property. He knew he had to act and act fast. If he failed to do either, the Tennessee Bureau of Investigation would do it for him.

Sheriff Johnsey told the newspaper all he could, gave the TV stations their soundbite for the evening news and promised everyone that this was not Islamic terrorism and that another press conference was imminent. He was discussing the possibility of a helicopter with a deputy when a tall white lady with sandy hair cropped behind her ears and wearing a gray suit and pink blouse approached him with a brown leather folder.

"Sheriff," she said, extending the dossier to him, "here is the roster for Introduction to American Literature, including Megan Fly."

Sheriff Johnsey frowned, sighed. "Thank you, Dr. Richardson." He opened the folder, thumbed through it.

Dr. Richardson cleared her throat. "There's one other thing. We have a policy that all cell phones must be turned off during class. Several people," she shielded her eyes from the sun, "myself included, have tried to contact everyone on the roster. We were able to reach the students who didn't come to class today. The red check marks by their names indicate that. The others, including Mrs. Fly, we believe to be in that classroom."

Sheriff Johnsey grimaced, grunted. He squinted as if his eyes were lasers boring a hole through the center of Dr. Richardson's head. He was agitated with everyone and everything: his fishing trip interrupted, reporters asking him the same questions, a fool waving a gun around a classroom and this college president trying to tell him something that he already knew. "Is there anything else we need to be aware of, Dr. Hamilton?"

"Van der Pool, Alexander van der Pool was a student here, briefly, seven years ago. We're searching the archives for his record now. And we also know that he created a disturbance on campus two weeks ago and your department was called."

"I'm fully aware of that. Thank you for all your cooperation and you have a great day." Sheriff Johnsey watched her walk away escorted by subordinates on both sides. He scratched the back of his neck, loosened a clod of dirt with a kick from the tip of his shoe and thought he saw the blinds move in the window that framed classroom 223A.

10

"Alright, van der Pool," Tobi said. *"You got everybody sitting around like we a bunch of Chinese flowers. We gone meditate or what? You better watch that motherfucker with the afro. He reminds me a lot of some of them niggers I used to hang out with at the pool hall."*

Alex eyed the afro who anchored the left side of the semi-circle. "What's your name?"

"Why?"

Alex rested the gun on his knee, his finger on the trigger.

"Monte. Monte Merriweather." He scowled, pronounced his name as though it were a dare.

Alex surveyed the others in the group from left to right who had fear where their eyes should've been, some visibly shaking. Next to Monte sat a brunette with bangs evenly trimmed across her forehead. She wore blue slacks, beige blouse and beneath her red sweater, Alex couldn't tell, but she looked like she was pregnant. Next to her was the redhead with the Muddy Waters t-shirt and to his left a man, gray-haired in his late fifties with a face clean-shaven wearing a light-green button-down shirt, had his arm around a woman in her early sixties sporting a pink baseball cap and an orange sweatshirt with Tennessee across the front.

Megan Fly sat in the middle of the semi-circle. "Alex, you said you had poetry. Can you read one?" Her voice inflected like a pair of raised eyebrows.

Alex stared at the woman in the ball cap sniffing back tears, wiping her eyes. He set the gun beside his leg, unwrinkled a sheet of paper from his book bag, looked around. "Where everybody at? Why the class so small?"

Megan smiled, explained, "We have six out for various reasons, mainly a virus. Four have left since you've been here. So, that leaves only us." She smiled again, making a bookend for her words

"If you ever wanted a captive audience, van der Pool, I don't think you could beat this group," Tobi remarked.

Alex nodded with understanding and held the sheet of paper at eye level, his free hand on the weapon. "This is called, 'OF TIME.'" He cleared his throat and began:

"Like before them and we,
And us those after,
Time is all and indifferent to us
It sweeps death into our river of mortality
Disposing memory fragments
Anonymity upon the shores,
The sea or Eternity, rushing.
It is time perpetual, time
It drives, controls us,
Often holds us denies, sometimes.
Precious sand of our hours
Have precisely been counted
Placed within a pre-destined end.
Time reveals not how.
Time reveals not when."

Alex raised his eyes from the paper, searched the faces of those before him for the slightest hint of approbation or derision, but found only blank stares from across the silence of the room.

"It's definitely original. A very sensitive poem."
It was the brunette with the bangs and red sweater.

11.

Every morning when Sara Carter awoke she had to throw up. The first two months there was very little morning sickness. Now, three months into the pregnancy the early morning trips to the bathroom had become routine, bending over the toilet, praying that it would end soon. After she'd washed her face, she would return back to bed and rest for another hour before a hot shower and preparation for class.

For the past two weeks, the little sleep she did get was disjointed like pieces of a jigsaw puzzle scattered across the floor. Only hearing from Nick would put the fragments together again. It had been two weeks now, two and a half actually since Sara had received a letter and they'd never gone that long without communicating with each other. The handwriting in his last letter had been more scribble than penmanship. It was as if Nick were writing in the dark or in a hurry before the lights were just about to be turned off. And some words like *Fallujah* and *Mosul* were almost illegible like he was nervous or the pen was in control of his hand. And now she stayed awake most nights staring at a picture of them together that she kept on the bedside table, praying that he was all right. He looked so handsome on that Sunday after church standing outside the restaurant the day of the photo. Captain of the high school football team, blonde, blue-eyed, broad-shouldered, he'd worn a gray suit and a red tie, his right arm gently draped around her waist. She, in a blue dress wearing the string of pearls inherited from her grandmother, stood by his side in the summer sun, had come to understand what love was for the very first time.

Sara traced the outline of Nick's face with her forefinger and wanted now more than anything in the world to be Mrs. Nicholas Matthews. Nick had talked of returning home, having a church wedding and working in the construction business with his father before striking out on his own. She'd never seen herself as his wife or anyone else's for that matter. But lately, the idea of it had become comfortable, like sitting before a fire on a cold winter's night. And the mere thought of the way he proposed never failed to bring a smile to her face, evoke eruptions of joy.

It was her 20th birthday and mutual friends of theirs had gathered for the evening to mark the occasion. The night belonged to dance, food, and music. And when it was time to pop the cork on the champagne, they serenaded her with the birthday song until she blushed, wishing her many more with a toast to health and prosperity. Nick had handed her a flute of libation and after the first sip, the sparkling wine tickled her nose until the glass was empty. Sara stared into the bottom of the glass, then at Nick and then at the other people in the room who were staring at her, smiling. With her index finger, she extracted a two carat diamond ring from the bottom of the glass and covered her mouth with her hand. She looked at Nick, but could only see the outline of his face through watery eyes.

"Will you marry me?" He was on one knee, her hand wrapped inside his, her answer voiced only by embracing him around the neck and a kiss upon the top of the head. When Nick got to his feet the whole room closed in upon the both of them with applause and hugs. Three months later he was in uniform and in the Middle East.

Sara held her hand at an angle allowing the engagement ring to catch the many facets of morning light. It was so beautiful. And so was Nick. She'd had friends who gotten pregnant by their boyfriends and their boyfriends had urged them to get rid of it, had become abusive or denied fatherhood altogether. But not Nick. When she told him she'd missed her period, he simply smiled and said he'd take care of everything. And he did. She just knew that their son would be like his daddy. Yes, son. She'd only wished Nick could've been there to view the results of the test, their baby sucking his thumb in the safety and warmth of her womb. And there would be others, kids, at least two more or so they had agreed upon. But all that seemed so far away now, like a balloon cut from its string floating skyward, a mere speck as far as the eye can see. It didn't matter how long it took him to come back to her, come back alive, Sara was determined to wait. What other options were at her disposal? The other alternative made her more nauseous than morning sickness and sent her body into cold convulsions. She no longer kept up with the war through the papers or evening news, but simply prayed the war over with soon and that they begin their lives together. Thank God for school and the distraction it provided. When Nick returned, he and the baby would occupy all of her time. But now college dominated her mind and its pursuits of a nursing degree blocked out thoughts of mental derangement, missing arms, and legs and flagged draped coffins. Sara loved her literature class and the poem Alex read reaffirmed what she had been feeling all along: there was nothing she could or couldn't do to get Nick home any sooner if she wanted to.

"I'm Sara." She half-waved, half-smiled. "And there's denseness to it as well."

Alex found a pen in his book bag, scribbled notes across the top of the paper.

"Sounds like the blues to me, which ain't nothing but philosophy. You a philosopher?"

Two hours ago, Brandon Whitby reached under the front seat and extracted a plastic bag half full of leafy green material. He stuck his nose into the substance and inhaled deeply, savoring its aroma like a wine taster sampling a vintage bottle from the vineyards of France. If he never exhaled again, he thought, that'd be all right with him. He'd paid twenty-five dollars the night before and it was a good score, no stems or seeds, just a nice dried healthy plant with a tint of brownish color. He could always count on Brasfield to come through with some good weed. He placed the bag of marijuana between his legs, then reached into the glove box, fumbling through insurance papers, registration slips, owner's manual and various personal papers become trash before securing with thumb and forefinger a yellow package of cigarette papers. He checked the rearview mirror and over both shoulders, then stuck two sheets of paper together, filling the seam with a generous amount of weed, rolling a tight well-formed joint and sealing the whole thing with a line of saliva.

He lit the cigarette and held the smoke in his lungs until he thought his face would explode. When he exhaled, a long aromatic mist filled the interior of the car with a sweet, intoxicating fragrance and Brandon was glad he was sitting down. If not, he would have staggered and fallen off his feet. There was nothing like a good smoke between classes. He checked over both shoulders again, surveying the parking lot and took another drag. Algebra II at 8 and Advanced Sophomore Literature at 11 a.m. After only two weeks of classes, he knew it wouldn't be long before he dropped Algebra II. It was just going to be too early in the morning, too much homework and too much hassle. Hell, I'm a musician. One semester is enough of that crap. Sophomore Lit. Now that was a little better, different anyway. That was art and he was an artist himself. He could get off on the poetry of Bob Dylan and T.S. Elliott and according to the syllabus, the short stories of Virginia Woolf and Fitzgerald and the essays of Baldwin and Mencken were to be read before semester's end. Besides, Professor Fly was cool. When she taught it was as though she took every word personally, like she was resurrecting the writer's words, breathing new life into them, words that Brandon had once considered dead and decaying.

But as much as he liked the Literature class, the World History, Sociology and of course Algebra had to go. Or maybe it was time for him to go. Sooner or later he was going to have to abandon all, including his parents' desire that he get a college degree, and totally devote himself to the one thing he cared about most in this world, music, the blues.

Jerry and Helen Whitby had plans for their only child to attend their alma mater and the place where they fell in love, Lee College in southeastern Tennessee to become a dentist like his father and his father before him. After days of conversations that ended in raised voices and nights punctuated with the slamming of doors, he found solace on the couches of friends who let him crashed until things cooled off. Stovall Community College wasn't a private religious based school halfway across the state, but it was college. Thus compromise and peace settled over the Whitby household once again.

Why do I have to listen to frustrated professors only there to pick up their pay twice a month when B.B. King, Robert Johnson, and Howling Wolf are the only teachers I'll ever need? And what's the point of showing up every day going through the same routine when the only classroom I want is a juke joint on stage with Roger and Bobby on drums and bass and the three of us singing Muddy Waters. I'm a blues musician that just happens to be a white boy. Or am I a white boy who just happens to be a blues musician? He would often tease himself and others with that question.

From the moment he'd heard Muddy Waters he'd known what he wanted to do with his life. He was twelve and looking for trouble and hanging out with friends at the mall rummaging discount CD bins of the music store, when he came across a "greatest hits" compilation. He'd strapped the headphones across his ears, pushed a couple buttons and when Muddy opened up on "Still a Fool" and began to wail the whole universe staggered. Brandon rushed home, babbling about guitars, lessons, concerts and more money to buy more CD's with old black men adorned on the covers. A month later he was taking guitar lessons from Mr. Jaco twice a week, pining the nights away in his room imitating the music he'd accumulated by the hundreds strewn across his bedroom floor.

The only thing Brandon loved more than music was his girlfriend of the past three years. And no matter how many times he repeated this, he couldn't convince himself that it was true. Even Kerri, a smart, ambitious, pretty, pre-law student at Princeton, Kerri was secondary when it came to the blues. When he was with her, he was thinking of the next gig, a record deal down the road or lyrics to his next song; she was the muse for over half the songs he'd written. He could hardly wait for the weekend. Kerri would be in town and this time of year was great for picnics, long walks or just doing nothing together. Or playing a gig down at Fishbones while she sat in the front row in a short black skirt with those big pretty legs crossed screaming as loud as she could each time he soloed.

Brandon put the joint to his lips and inhaled, but the fire had gone out. It didn't matter. He was ready for class now. He tossed the roach into the ashtray, brushed wayward ashes from his clothes, smiled and nodded to himself in the rearview mirror. Yeah, it was always a good time for the blues.

"I'm Brandon. But everybody calls me Tennessee Red." The red curls piled atop his head certified the sobriquet. "I'm a bluesman."

"You hear that bullshit, van der Pool? What the hell a white boy know about the blues? Ask me about Robert Johnson, Blind Lemon Jefferson or the original Sonny Boy Williamson and I can tell you what they told me: ain't nothing romantic about the blues. Ain't nothing romantic about being broke or hungry or sick or being a long way from home and not knowing if you'll ever get back or even know the way back. Ain't nothing romantic about losing a woman or not being able to have a relationship with one. And hard living brings with it hard loving. A lot of people don't understand that the blues is a way of life. Hard life. This country gave us a hard life and we made the blues out of it. Made some kind of life out of it. And this redhead guy, he reminds me a lot of somebody. Somebody, I don't like. Say he's a bluesman, huh? If he got the blues, he stole 'em. I got a feeling that he think the blues romantic too. And they might be for him 'cause when he get tired or bored of playing his guitar or whatever he plays loud and long enough wherever he plays them, he can walk off that stage when he gets good and ready any time he good and ready and still be white."

"How you know so much about the blues, Tobi?"

"Man, you can measure my whole life by 12 bars in 4/4 time."

"I hear ya," Alex said. "But as far as music goes or any kind of art for that matter, once you create it and put it out there, everybody owns it. The whole world has the blues today. And one day they'll have my poetry too."

"Van der Pool. You ain't been around as long as I thought you have. Robert Johnson ain't got paid yet."

Alex looked at Brandon as though he'd dropped through the tiled ceiling, had laid eyes on him for the first time.

"I'm a poet, man. Don't know much about philosophy," he said and the name Camus flashed from his sister's bookshelf. Alex was about to say how much he liked the blues and that he really loved jazz even more when the walls began to speak his name in acoustic, amplified tones. When they mouthed his name again, he closed his eyes, laid the pistol by his side and resigned himself to the fact that this was it, that God was coming to take him to heaven just as fast as He could. But when the voice spoke a third time it came from beyond the walls with a southern drawl and a Tennessee twang and Alex opened his eyes with a start, grabbed his pistol prepared to shoot his way out of hell. He looked at his captives looking between him and the window like spectators at a tennis match. "Don't move."

He pushed himself up, fingered an opening between blinds. He looked out among the crowd behind barricades that swelled before his eyes. Alex narrowed his vision upon the white-haired man in a green vest with a black megaphone in his mouth pointing it at him as though it were a high-powered rifle. He ducked when he heard his name fired again.

"Alexander van der Pool. This is Sheriff Warren Johnsey. I need you to answer Megan Fly's phone. We need to talk." His words floated upon the air, became entangled among limbs of trees. "Alexander van der Pool?"

Alex whipped around, questioned Megan Fly without saying a word.

"My phone's in my purse," she answered, anticipated the next query by the frown on his face. "It's turned off. School policy to cut down on cheating, among other things."

Alex slid his back down the wall until his butt rested on the floor. He rubbed his bald head with both hands trying to make answers magically appear or sort out the various voices in his ear. Tobi was asking how does someone get a phone in their purse, Megan Fly insisted that she had to answer that phone and Sheriff Johnsey droned his name in metallic syllables, wanted to know if he could hear him at all. And when his hostages began to raise the decibels of their murmurs into complaints, all the voices merged as one, stuck in Alex's right temple as a throbbing pain.

"Lady, will you get that fucking phone!"

Megan scurried behind her desk, unzipped a designer purse and retrieved a smartphone that was ringing as she cut it on. "Megan Fly. Yes. I think we're alright. Yes. Just a minute." She walked towards Alex and extended the phone as though it were a handshake.

With a wave of his gun, Alex motioned her to rejoin the others. "Hello? Yeah. Who this? Sheriff Johnsey?"

"Before we start talking, I need to know if anyone is hurt. We need to get anybody to a doctor?"

"Sheriff Johnsey?" Alex felt all the blood in his body rush to his head. "You remember me, motherfucker?"

"Is anybody hurt, son?"

"Do you remember me?"

"Yes, son. I remember you."

"Well, I'm hurt goddammit. I got the stitches to prove it."

The Sheriff turned his back as though he were having a private conversation. "The administration asked you to leave the campus Alex, and when I asked you to do so, you refused again and I had no other choice but to physically remove you."

"You hit me with that nightstick! You could've put my fucking eye out."

"I tried to handcuff you and you resisted arrest, son. Once it gets to that point, you don't control what happens."

"You know good and goddam well I never resisted," Alex screamed. "Why don't you tell another lie? You seem to be good at it. Why don't you tell everybody that I tried to go for your weapon or that I fit the description? That way the next time you shoot down an unarmed black man in the streets, you'll already have an excuse handy."

"Son. That's over and done with. We're in this pond right here right now. We gotta talk."

"Everybody's good, man," Alex interrupted him. "But, why you think I want to talk to you?"

"We need to work it out. We *got* to work it out, Alex. It'll be better for you to deal with me than to deal with the guys I have to deal with. I'm a patient man, but they're not."

"Do me a favor?"

"I'll see what I can do. What is it?

"Don't call me son."

The Sheriff chuckled. "I can do that. Tell me what you want Alex?"

"Poetry."

"Poetry? What is poetry?"

"Man, if you got to ask, I doubt if you'll ever find out," Alex smiled, hung up the phone.

"Monte cleared his throat. "Yo, dog. I need to answer my phone, too? There's an important call I need to make. Don't y'all need to answer y'all phones?" He addressed the other hostages, his eyes pleading, his voice imploring.

"Van der Pool. What the hell is that thing, man?

Alex flipped the phone vertically, then horizontally. "It's a smartphone, Tobi. You can do any damn thing you want to with it. Call somebody, find directions, watch a movie and anything in between." He rotated the phone a second time and the picture on the screen rotated with it. "You never heard of a smartphone?"

"Hey man. I'm the twentieth-century distortion of your imagination. What the fuck I need with a cell phone? But I'll be damned. Back in the day, we got into trouble 'cause we didn't have enough shit. Y'all can get into trouble because y'all got too much shit. Look like the phone smarter than the ones using it. How anybody ever get anything done hooked up to a machine like that all day?"

Alex shook his head. "You got it twisted, Tobi. How anybody ever get anything done if they are *not* hooked up to one of these things is the question."

"So where your phone at?"

"I had one . . ." Alex trailed off. "Caroline . . . . ."

"Who's Caroline, van der Pool?"

"That was my girl. We had a fight."

"Oh, yeah. You was supposed to tell me about her. Remember?"

"Not now, Tobi."

"Yo, dog. I need to make a call." Monte interrupted the conversation in Alex's head. "I got to talk to a man that need to talk to me."

Alex handed the phone back to Megan, took his seat at the head of the semi-circle. He looked Megan squarely in the eye. "Before I came in, I heard you talking about Langston Hughes. What about him?"

The phone rang with an urgency that knocked it

from Megan's hand. She picked it up, looked at Alex and when he nodded his approval, answered it. It was Sheriff Johnsey demanding to speak with Alex.

"Tell 'im I'll talk to him later after we get through talking about Langston. I ain't going nowhere and he ain't either."

Megan didn't have to repeat the instructions; Alex had shouted them halfway across the room. "What about him?" he repeated.

"Well," Megan sighed, "we were going to discuss in detail one of Hughes' poems: "The Negro Speaks of Rivers." Will that be ok?"

The sun rose from one corner of Alex's smile to the other, left his face with a golden iridescence.

"I have copies of the poem on my desk. May I pass them out?"

"Be careful, van der Pool. Everybody's got their eye on that door. I seen 'em."

Alex was on his feet, stood between her and the door as she collected a blue folder from her desk. Megan passed out the poem, kept one for herself. "Alex. Would you read it for the class?"

He looked from face to face, shook his head. "No. I've read one poem. Let somebody else read."

"Alex," Megan's voice slapped him on the back of the hand. "This is a literature class where we read, discuss, write about and sometimes write short stories and poetry. You wanted to be in the class. You're in the class. This is your class now. Could you do us the honor of reading 'The Negro Speaks of Rivers?'"

Alex held his gun with one hand, poetry with the other and swallowed. He read as though he were a high priest reciting a sacred text calling the faithful to worship.

"Very good, Alex. Thank you," Megan Fly smiled. "All right class. We'll talk more about the structure of the poem later, but for now, let's start with the opening line: *I've known rivers.* Would anyone like to comment on that? Mr. Strother?"

Mr. Strother was the gray-haired man in his late fifties with the clean shaven face wearing a button down light green shirt. "Reminds me of what my daddy said once when he was talking about D-Day." A distant look swept across his eyes. "He lost an arm storming the beach that day, but left a lot more than that behind. Said 'he'd known wars.' And I believed him. It wasn't something he'd read in a book or saw in a movie or heard by word of mouth. He knew war the way you know a lover. That war broke his heart and he never got over it."

"Thank you, Mr. Strother. 'I've known rivers ancient as the world and older than the. Mrs. Verdell?'"

Mrs. Verdell looked from Megan to Alex before staring down at her paper. "Could be the beginning of the *Iliad* or the *Odyssey*. Anyway, sounds like the start of an epic poem. Or something on a grand scale anyway." Ruby Verdell, in her early sixties, sported a pink baseball cap and an orange sweatshirt with Tennessee blazoned across the front. She had dried her tears and blown her nose with a handkerchief that belonged to Mr. Strother, who graciously insisted that she keep it in case of future emergencies.

Megan smiled in her direction. "Yes. It does have a larger than life appeal to it. Good. Monte. 'Flow of human blood in human veins?'"

Monte scratched his afro, combed it back into place with the palm of his hand. "I don't know. I don't know a lot about the Bible, but that could've come from the Bible. Since you asked me."

"Thank you, Monte. Not only that line, but the whole poem has a spiritual tone to it, as though it's a sacred text found in a religious book. Very good. Are there any questions?" The class looked at one another, then back at their papers.

"'My soul has grown deep like the rivers.' Alex?"

Alex hesitated, stammered, started again. "Rivers have been around a long time and sounds like the old man has, too."

"That's interesting, Alex," Megan smiled as if she swallowed a warm juicy secret. "How do you know it's an old man? You think it could be an old woman?"

He frowned at the prospect, hunched his shoulders. "Maybe so . . . I thought since a man wrote it . . ."

"What about the idea," Megan pressed her forefinger against her lips, "that's it's both male and female. In other words, the 'I' in the poem is a collective 'we' and instead of the poem speaking for one particular person, it speaks for a race of people."

"Mrs. Fly," Sara said, "I always thought that the speaker in the poem was Time itself. The only person who's been around as long as the rivers themselves is God. And God is a spirit."

"Oh. That's a great observation, Sara. But with the use of poetic license, time becomes part of the collective voice and as Alex alluded to, not only is the poet black, but let's look at some of the cultural references he utilizes to strengthen the collective voice as well . . . Brandon . . . Can you comment on the next two lines?"

'I bathed in the Euphrates when dawns were young/I built my hut near the Congo and it lulled me to sleep.'

Brandon laughed. "I wish I would've wrote 'em. Would've made some great blues lyrics. The poem is narrower now that he names specific rivers. I know the Congo's in Africa. Not sure about the Euphrates."

"Tigris and Euphrates," Mr. Strother added. "Two

of the oldest rivers in the history of the world, Red. Located in Iraq or thereabouts. That's in the Bible, too."

"And I believe, I could be wrong, but I don't think so, that Hughes was aware of the connection between the Bible and history too when he wrote this poem. Remember, science records that the remains of the oldest humans were found on the continent of Africa and one of the earliest civilizations was established around the Tigris and Euphrates, which if viewed on a map, especially an ancient map, is in very close proximity to one another. So, I think the collective voice is really taking shape in the poem. Especially, in light of the next four lines."

'I looked upon the Nile and raised the pyramids above it/I heard the singing of the Mississippi when Abe Lincoln/went down to New Orleans, and I've seen its muddy/bosom turn all golden in the sunset.'

"Now, "Megan elaborated, "if I didn't know what color Hughes was, the references in these lines would give it away. The Nile's in Egypt and Egypt's in Africa and I think history bears out there were Black dynasties during the time the pyramids were built . . ."

"*Van der Pool?*

"Yeah, Tobi?"

'First this white boy and the blues and now this white woman and black history. You know you in trouble when white folks starting explaining who you are, what you do and why you do it. Next thing you know, they'll have you believing you're a fucking Chinese. Matter of fact, I think Meagan and Tennessee Red might be Communists, too. Why you think they call him 'red'? And another thing: They ain't got no black folks that can teach black poetry?"

"I'm sure they have, Tobi. But just 'cause you black don't mean you gonna get it right or want to get it right. This woman handling this poem like she respects it, like it gives her some kind of joy she just can't keep to herself. All this woman care about is truth. I don't care what color she is. You ever met a white person you could trust, Tobi?

"Van der Pool. I ain't never met nobody I could trust."

" . . . and as has been pointed out, look how Hughes narrows his focus through the Mississippi which represents repression and bondage to Abe Lincoln, the great emancipator—"

"Great emancipator? You hear that, van der Pool? You waiting on somebody to free you, you'll end up getting used to those damn chains and won't even know you wearing them anymore. You got to take freedom wherever you find it, even if it's around the throat, man. And it ain't no one time thing either. You gonna have to fight for the rest of your life. You already know."

"—and what happens when Lincoln was 21 years old? I'm glad you asked. He took a boat ride down the Mississippi and got a firsthand account of the conditions slaves had to endure. So without a doubt, Hughes wrote this poem in the collective voice of the African American or as the title states, the Negro. So," Megan looked at the poem as though it were a long-lost friend, "the poem concludes similarly to the way it opened. But this time, Hughes chooses the word 'dusky.' How does that affect the poem? How did it affect you?"

The mechanical hum of an air conditioner vibrated the silence in the room.

"Alex?"

Alex looked up and found everyone looking at him. He made a *hmmm* sound under his breath. "It adds a rhythm to the writing . . ."

". . . Go on," Megan prodded.

"It's almost like," Alex's heard someone strike a match in his head and he could see things he'd never seen before, "like the poem is finished but not finished, makes a complete circle of itself."

"Oh, that's good, Alex. So, Hughes' choice of the word *dusky*, what does that do for the poem?"

Sara placed her elbow on her knee, rested her chin on her fist. "I don't know if I agree that the poem makes a circle or not. But I do know the word *dusky* seems to mark an end. He starts the poem off with dawn and finishes it with dusk and so it feels like he said all he wanted to say."

"The speaker has to be a man, Mrs. Fly" interrupted Mr. Strother. "The person at the end of this poem sounds tired, the way my daddy used to when he got through talking about the war, as if he were reliving it every time he told it. And I guess he was."

"Well," Mrs. Fly took the reins of the discussion once again," those are two excellent points to be noted. And the sun has yet to fail to rise each morning, so as Alex pointed out, there's a continuation, a self-sustaining nature to the poem and Hughes has managed to capture time, history and a peoples' perspective in a twenty-four hour period." She paused to catch her breath and was about to say that it was a remarkable poem when the phone rang from the floor between her knees. Megan looked at Alex. "It's the Sheriff."

"See what he wants."

"He wants to know what you want." She slid the phone across the floor to Alex.

"Alex? Sheriff Johnsey. This Langston fellow . . . he in on this thing with you?"

"I guess you could say that," Alex laughed.

Anger rose in Sheriff Johnsey's voice. "Where can we find him? We know he's not in the room with you"

"Not anymore." Alex was laughing without sound.

"Where is he, Alex?"

"Try Harlem." Alex covered the mouthpiece with

his hand and addressed the class. "I told him where to find Langston." Megan and Red laughed, Sara smiled, Monte nodded, Mr. Strother shook his head and Mrs. Verdell raised her eyebrows.

Sheriff Johnsey's anger dissipated into dead air on the other end of the line. "All right, Alex. I hear people laughing in the background, so the joke's on me. That's fine. I have a sense of humor. And I tell you what, since we're all in a pretty good mood right now, why don't we call all this nonsense off?"

"Ain't no-nonsense, Sheriff. This is life or death."

"I'm well aware of that fact, son. But all this ain't making no sense for you, me, the folks you holding or anybody else. I need to know what you want. A few minutes ago, you told me you wanted poetry. But hell, I've been thinking, you could've had poetry without doing all this. So I need you to tell me what you really want, Alex? That's what I'm here for."

Alex removed the phone from his ear, rolled his eyes toward the ceiling. "Man, I asked you a minute ago why you think I want to talk to you and you ain't give me an answer yet."

"You all I got, Alex and there ain't no one else for you to talk to. I don't have a problem talking because this is the time for it. But it's bound to get late sooner or later and there won't be anything left to say. At this point, we're all we got. We got to work this thing out where nobody gets hurt, man. Tell you what . . ." Sheriff Johnsey coughed, cleared this throat, "if you don't know what you want, why don't you just lay your weapons down and walk out the door with your hands up and that'll be that and I'll be at the door with my hands up to make sure you don't get hurt. To make sure neither one of us don't get hurt. Alex?"

Alex's eyes rested on Mrs. Verdell with her hand

raised in the air holding up a pressing need. "It's past time for me to take my medicine. I can't do it on an empty stomach."

Alex nodded, spoke into the phone. "OK, Sheriff. Tell you what I want: Let me get some pizzas. What kind? I don't know, man. Just five or six pizzas. And some sodas. And a few chocolate chip cookies. No. That's it."

All right, Alex. I got it. Give me about thirty minutes. By the way, your mother is here."

"My mama? Where?" His heartbeat pounded in his throat.

"She's here with me, Alex. Your mom and stepdad. They want to talk to you, Alex."

The phone almost slipped through his fingers. He switched it to his other hand. "I don't want to talk to nobody. Why you bring them down here, man?"

"I ain't brought nobody nowhere. They came down here on their own. Your family cares about you, Alex. Your sister Margaret's here too."

Alex's temples throbbed. "That shit ain't cool, Sheriff."

"All right. Your problem ain't with me, now. I'm just doing what you tell me to do. Let me get you some eats and we'll go from there. OK?"

Alex hung up the phone, watched the backlit screen fade to black.

"Thank you." He recognized Mrs. Verdell's voice without looking up and when he did she was smiling at him. "And I like your poem a lot."

'Time reveals not how/Time reveals not when.'

17

Rose Verdell removed her pink cap. Alex's mouth dropped open. Her head was clean shaven and where his shined from applying lotion, hers had a faint glow. But those lines hung in the air for Rose long after Alex had read them. They reminded her why she was enrolled at Stovall State to begin with. She awoke one morning to discover that everyone and everything was gone. Everything she'd known or taken for granted unrecognizable, everything she'd cherished just a pile of ashes. She'd been so busy living that she'd missed out on life. Married at sixteen to the same man for 40 years. During that time, she was Mrs. Don Verdell, devoted wife at the Baptist Church, the PTA and Boy Scouts, nurtured five kids on her breasts and at her hip. Between ironing, cooking and cleaning, there was the occasional new dress or a Saturday night at the movies. But usually, the sun rose with the life of her children and when it didn't, it set on her husband, his coming home frustrated five out of six days a week from Hoswell Manufacturing Plant, grumbling about bosses and unions or worst: not speaking to her or anyone about anything. As long as she stayed buried in the lives of others, she didn't know that she needed air or that she was even conscious of breathing. But first there was Adam and Frank, then Linda and Cynthia and finally Jake. One by one, on to college, then marriage and kids and lives of their own until one winter morning Rose awoke to a heavy silence and the vastness of space. The rooms in the house seemed bigger and Don always beyond her reach, even though they shared the same bed.

Two years ago, she received a call around 2 p.m. on a Monday afternoon that Don had been rushed to the emergency room and when she got there, he was already gone. He'd grabbed his chest on the assembly line in that plant and died of a heart attack en route to the hospital. After the funeral, when family and friends had departed, food and flowers packed away, she sat in Don's favorite chair counted her own breaths. Every time she inhaled, she became puzzled about where her life had gone and when she exhaled she wondered where and how to find it. It seemed like it took her a year to get out of that chair and when she did Adam and Jake wanted her to pack up, sell the house and leave Stovall to stay with either of them. But then Linda's question followed her around like a stray pet: What is it you've always wanted to do, Mama, that you've never had the time to do? She pondered her daughter's query and pursued the answer by joining a book club, studying tai chi, taking up tennis, learning to crochet and enrolling in classes at the Adult Enrichment Center to attain a GED. Going to that Center three days a week created a spark in her not to only attain a piece of paper, but became a conflagration towards anything that had to do with learning. The possible consumed Rose and she found herself studying when she didn't even have homework. Around the holiday table, her other children's voices rose in chorus about college. She pressed her hands to her ears to block out their song, but refrains of their pleas slipped through her fingers. They would pay the full tuition for her to go to the University of Tennessee, their alma mater. But instead of going all the way across the State, Stovall State was just across town and encouraged adult learners. The University of Tennessee was a big school with a big student body that she knew was a lot smarter than herself. But after making the Dean's List for the first semester of her freshman year, she felt like a kid learning to ride a bike without training wheels, even as she was falling against the pavement to bruise and cut herself. Two months ago, one morning after showering, she detected a lump in her right breast. A biopsy confirmed its malignancy and after two rounds of chemotherapy, radiation, and prescription pills, she'd lost two breasts, ten pounds and all the hair on her head. But she was determined not to lose any more time. "Time reveals not how/Time reveals not when." Cancer or no cancer, chemo or no chemo, she'd become accustomed to the wind on her face and the freedom it brought with it, that this was her time to go as far as her legs would take her. But still, some days declarations to graduate from Harvard or Yale sat on one shoulder. Other days, questions of whether she even belonged at a junior college sat on the other.

Rose put the cap back on her head. All she knew was that two more rounds of chemo awaited her future, that there was a Black man who kept talking to himself sitting directly opposite her with a wild look in his eye, a knife and gun in either hand. She resolved that all of this was a mere toll she had to pay to be on her way.

"Yo, dog?"

Alex lifted his eyes without raising his head.

"Yo, dog?" Monte said.

Alex gripped his pistol, laid it on his lap. "Yeah. What's up, man?"

Monte was twisting the front of his afro into baby dreadlocks. "Man, I really need to get to my phone right now. There's a school down in Florida that's thinking about offering me a scholarship. If I don't hear from them, they definitely need to hear from me."

"What kind of scholarship," Alex frowned.

For the first time, Monte smiled. "I'm centerfield, dog. Number 25. Bats left, throws right. All-District and All-State out of Ridgedale High. Everybody wanted me coming out of high school."

"What the hell you doing here?"

Monte reveled in telling the story as if he were on the witness stand and the whole court rapt. He leaned forward into the tale. "State championship game my junior year. We were in Murfreesboro, down by two in the bottom of the sixth. Men on third and second. I'm at the plate and I'm swinging with a 3-2 count. I rip one over the third baseman's head and it's down the line in left field. I'm cruising around first about to trot to a stand up double looking cool as hell like I should be on the cover of GQ or something. But I check left field again and the left fielder is Tommy Breland. He's All-American too and the reason why is that he got an AK for an arm and he done wound up like he on the pitcher's mound about to shoot me down at second base. So, I get back on my horse, but I can see the seams on that baseball as it's coming faster and faster my way. I'm DOA, dog and I know it. But I slide when I slide and everything moves except this right knee." He thumped the air towards his knee with his index finger. "It pops, cracks, pens itself under my right leg. They say they could hear it all the way up in the bleachers. I don't doubt it. That sound still wakes me up sometimes in the middle of the night. After that, the phone stopped ringing, the mailman didn't drop off no more letters and no college coaches stopped by the house to promise me what all they could do for me if I came to their universities. So, I didn't play none my senior season. The doctors rebuilt the knee and I spent the whole year rehabbing and getting my shit together. Last year I walked on here at Stovall and had a pretty good season. I'm not back to where I was before I blew my knee, but I'm damn close, which makes me good enough to be better than most guys with two good knees. Florida State recruited me hard when I was in high school and they're the only ones who want to give me a second chance."

Monte's slowed his breathing until it became deep and reflective. He focused on a spot on the wall just above Alex's head.

"I learned a lot when I got hurt, dog," he continued. "The main thing I learned was that I'm just a piece of meat. I'm the prey and when the predators get enough of me or I don't have anything left to give, they'll toss me on the side of the road and leave the rest for the buzzards. Then they go searching for fresh meat." He narrowed his vision back upon Alex. "I ain't no poet. I'm a jock and I know how the game's played. And that's exactly what I'm gonna do. I'm gonna use them as much as they use me. Florida State's my only chance to get away from Stovall and not end up in one of these factories or in jail around here. That's why I need to get to my phone and check that email. You got my life in your hands. But that college in Tallahassee holds my future."

The more Alex looked at Monte the more his cheekbones, eyes and lips reminded him of someone. He was about to ask if he were related to a Leon Merriweather, a high school All-State football performer and his classmate from seven years ago, when the phone rang. Alex glanced at the phone in his hand, then at Monte. "You'll get to use your phone, man." He panned the semi-circle from left to right. "Everybody'll get to use their phone. OK?"

"Hello?"

"Alex?"

"Yeah."

Sheriff Johnsey's sounded light and rosy over the phone. "One of my guys will be outside your door in five minutes with the pizza."

"Sheriff?"

"Yeah, Alex?"

Alex's voice was solemn and opaque. "Don't fuck with me."

"What are you talking about, son?"

He screeched like fingernails clawing a chalkboard. "Don't fuck with me, man!"

Sheriff Johnsey almost screamed back into the phone, but fell silent. When he spoke his words were a salve. "Alex. You asked for pizza and sodas. I got you pizza and soda. Now, I got a guy—one of my deputies, unarmed—standing outside the door waiting for you to let him in. He'll set the pizzas down, make sure everybody's all right and then turn around and leave."

"I got a gun." Alex was deliberate, liked the way it felt. "I got a knife and a gun and seven other folks in here with me. You trying to get somebody killed? You trying to get yourself killed? Anybody that's comes thought that goddam door's a dead man."

"Wait a minute, Alex . . . you're saying that there are seven people in the room with you?"

Alex knew Tobi was not the distortion of his imagination. He knew he was the only one he could truly talk to. He didn't care what anyone said. Tobi was real. "I meant six, sheriff. You know what the hell I meant."

Sheriff Johnsey made sucking sounds through his teeth. "I really didn't, Alex. That's why I need you to let one of my guys come in and check things out. I can have him strip down to his underwear, if that'll make you happy."

"No. Nobody gets in the room. I got a lady that needs to take her medicine and can't do it on an empty stomach. Other than that, everybody's ok. If they weren't, you'd know it by now. Besides, if I wanted to hurt somebody, they would've been hurt a long time ago." Alex waved his weapon in the direction of the hostages.

"If you got somebody sick, maybe you need to let her go like you did the other two. You don't want somebody sick dying on your conscience, do you?"

"Don't fuck with me, Sheriff. Nobody in the room and nobody out. That part of the conversation's over."

Sheriff Johnsey cleared his throat. "All right. What do you want, Alex?"

"I want you to leave the food outside the door and then I want to talk to my mama. Where is she?"

"You got everybody here, man. You looked out the window lately? All the big boys are here: *CNN, FOX, ABC. The Times, The Herald, The Examiner.* Everybody wants to know what you want. What *do* you want, Alex?"

"Where's my mama?"

"She's right here. We're going to get you some help. OK?"

"Put her on the phone," he demanded.

"The pizzas are outside the door getting cold, Alex. I don't want Ms. Verdell getting sick on us. You need anything else, call me. Enjoy your meal."

"Sheriff Johnsey? How you know Mrs. Verdell's the one that's sick? Sheriff Johnsey?"

Alex stared into the phone as if he could see the silence on the other end. He pressed the phone to his forehead, squeezed his eyes shut and moved his lips without words falling from them. When there was a scuffle of sound outside the door, he jumped to his feet. Alex dropped the cell phone and it landed with a thud against the floor. The only thing wilder than the look in his eye was the pistol waving his right hand. "Hey. What's your name again?" He pointed the gun at the center of her forehead.

"Sara," she hesitated as if unsure of her own name.

"Get up. Everybody else . . . stay down."

He marched Sara towards the door with the barrel of the pistol resting against the base of her skull. Halfway across the room, Sara stopped, looked over her left shoulder and into Alex's eyes. "I'm not going to try anything."

Alex motioned with his free hand for her to keep walking and open the door. "Slowly." When they reached the door, Sara opened it and Alex made himself as small as possible behind her. When she stepped into the hall to retrieve the food and drink, he pressed his back to the doorframe inside the room, one eye on her, the other down the hallway, the gun vacillating between the two.

Sara handed Alex two bags and took her same spot in the semi-circle. He slammed the door shut with his foot and set the food in the midst of them. In one bag, he removed six large pizzas and from the other came sodas, plates, napkins, knives and forks.

"Mind if we bless the food?" asked Mr. Strother.

The voice startled Alex.

"Don't let 'em do it, van der Pool. Who the hell is we? If he wanna bless the food, let him bless his own damn food. He don't need to bless mine."

Alex looked askance, spoke out of the side of his mouth. "I didn't know you was eating, Tobi." He turned towards Mr. Strother. "No, sir. I don't mind. Go ahead and bless the food."

"Heavenly Father," Mr. Strother coughed, dislodged whatever was in his throat. "Thank You for your grace, your mercy and your provision. Thank You for this day and all that is good within it. Thank You for the many blessings You've given us and those yet to come. We now pray that this food be nourishment for our bodies and thank You for the ones who have prepared it. In your son Jesus' name." The word "amen" echoed and faded from the room.

Mr. Strother bit into a slice of sausage and pepperoni and grimaced when the cheese burned the roof of his mouth. He formed his lips into the shape of an O and began to blow until he was able to swallow. He glanced at the others in the room, sipped from the soft drink in front of him. That always seemed to happen whenever he ate pizza, he smiled. He wiped his mouth with a napkin, carefully took another bite and watched Alex squat in a distant corner, mumbling to himself. Alex was taller, but not as heavy as Lionel Spann and they both had clean-shaven heads. The more Mr. Strother chewed the more Lionel Spann came to mind.

15

When Robert Strother interviewed for the assembly line at Telmark Foods seventeen years ago, Lionel Spann was the interviewer. Spann was Human Resources manager and when he extended his hand across an oak desk after a forty-five minute interview, Strother began work the very next day. For five years, he ran a machine that slapped the Telmark label on cans of pork-n-beans and for the next five years, he operated a machine that arranged those cans in boxes to be shipped all over the country. Strother was good to Telmark Foods: he usually arrived early, never missed a day, found little to complain about and was the first one to volunteer for overtime. When whispers of unions rumbled through the plant, it was Strother who knocked on Spann's door one Friday afternoon and informed him of the where, how, when and who were speaking what about such sinister plots. And Telmark was good to Robert Strother: for the next five years he served under Spann, now Plant Manager, as line supervisor, purchased himself a bigger house on the edge of the suburbs, allowed his wife, Carol, to become a stay at home Mom, was about to graduate one daughter from college and send the other off to a private school next year. There were family vacations, a BMW, a 401k and plans for retirement until Telmark Foods became Hunter Products of Ohio a year later.

One Friday afternoon, Spann called Strother into his office, informed him that Hunter no longer had a need for shift supervisors when a machine could do the job. Spann thanked him for his years of service, assured him that if it were his call it wouldn't go down like this, but there was nothing he could do. With a handshake, Strother walked across the parking lot, got into his vehicle and drove home. Carol knew that something wasn't right as soon as he walked through the door and when she asked what was wrong, he laid a month's severance pay on the kitchen table, went into the bathroom, closed the door behind him and cried. He simply couldn't believe and from time to time, he still thought about it. He despised the Unions, any Unions because of the experience his own father had had with them. Any chance Robert had to stop them at the door and to keep them out of the plant, he'd take advantage of. He figured management would be grateful and would have his back to show their appreciation. But it wasn't the Unions who stabbed him in the heart. It was the people he trusted most. The ones who left him to wallow in his own blood.

A few days later, he was certain that with his work ethic and experience, he'd be punching someone's time clock within a month. But nine months later the unemployment benefits were gone and the 401k was going fast. Half of the manufacturing plants in west Tennessee were padlocking their doors and setting up shop in Mexico. The other half weren't hiring, especially middle-aged middle managers without a college degree. Since he'd been out of work for the past year, he wasn't even middle class anymore. He, Carol and Amber his youngest all had to move in with his in-laws since they now owed more on the house than what it was worth; the BMW was traded for a Chevy. Chelsea, his oldest, had to apply for student loans to finish her senior year at the University of Alabama and if Amber didn't score high enough on the ACT her schooling would be administered at the hand of a state college. For the past six months, Carol had become receptionist for a downtown lawyer specializing in divorce and for a while Strother thought that they would have to utilize his services. They fought over the most trivial of things, not because she was employed and the breadwinner, but because he was unemployed and didn't know what to do about it.

Last month, one evening after supper, Strother received a phone call from Lionel Spann, wanted to know if he was interested in a Chamber of Commerce program to train unemployed and underemployed workers. Job placement was the reward that dangled from the end of the program. A week later Robert Strother enrolled in Stovall State Community College to pursue an Associate degree in Business Administration. He was determined to catch up with that piece of paper, squeeze it as tight as he could until a new job, another house, a bigger car, the relationship he had with his wife and kids and the life that he used to know fell from it.

Lionel Spann. Mr. Strother chewed the last of his pizza, gulped it down with soda and wiped his mouth. He stared at Alex as if he wasn't even in the room and suddenly remembered that he never thanked Lionel for pulling the right strings to get him into the program. He vowed that when all this mess was over, besides kissing his wife and kids, it would be one of the first things he did.

"Tobi? Tobi? Where you at?"

"I'm right here, van der Pool."

"Where you been?" Alex had opened a box, removed a slice of pizza and had fixed his mouth to shove half of it inside.

"I've been everywhere and I've been nowhere . . . Look here, van der Pool. I wouldn't eat that if I was you."

Alex stopped the pizza inches from his lips as if he were frozen in time. "Why not?"

"Probably because they want you to. You dealing with white folks, van der Pool. Most of the time when you do what they don't expect you to, you'll be alright. Remember that."

Alex held the pizza at arm's length, scrutinized it with one eye shut, grunted and dropped it back into the box. When he looked up, Mr. Strother was looking into his mouth and down his throat as if he were trying to examine his tonsils. "What you looking at, man? " Alex's words snapped against the ear of Mr. Strother who blinked his way out of a trance, mumbled, "nothing" and brushed crumbs from his lap.

Soda cans opening, lips smacking were the only sounds. Red belched and apologized.

"Tobi?"

"Yeah, van der Pool."

"What you got against God?"

"I ain't got nothing against God?"

"You didn't want that man to pray over the food."

"I ain't got nothing against prayer either. Depends on who's

doing the praying, though. Something ain't right about that guy over there, van der Pool. He know all the words. But, hell, I could pray, too, if I had a gun in my face. As far as God goes, I believe there's a God. I just ain't never bothered Him for nothing. After He left me alone, I left Him alone."

"When did God ever leave you alone, Tobi?"

"The day I was born poor and Black. I want some of heaven where I'm living and while I'm living. But all I've ever known of this earth is hunger, cold and lack and I can't make all that fit with waiting until I died and everything would then be all right up in the clouds somewhere. See, that's for suckers and it's a trick white folks done brainwashed niggers to believe for years. Niggers been brainwashed so long, they don't need white folks to do it to them anymore. We can do it to ourselves better than any white folks ever could. But it ain't just niggers. Any religion anywhere that string anybody along like that is just another form of dope. Don't matter if you hyped up or nodding off all the time. As long as you're numb and can't feel anything that's when you know you got good religion. But it's ok, van der Pool. I ain't never asked nobody for no sympathy and I stopped being a victim la ong time ago. I do what I do and I own up to it. Folks think I'm scared, but I ain't never been scared of nothing. As far as that pie in the sky stuff goes, I been hungry, but not that hungry. I ain't got nothing against God, van der Pool. I figured if I was gonna suffer, I'd give Him a break. I could do that on my own."

"Tobi. We gonna have to deal with Jesus Christ. Ain't no way around it. We can either carry the body now or carry it later. But either way, that body has got to be thrown over your shoulder. You understand what I'm saying to you?"

"You got me on that one."

Alex sat up straight. "Jesus is God and God is truth and that's the body we got to bear. It'll either crush you or set you free. Where we carry it to and what we do with it when we get there, that's another story."

"Think you got it all mixed up, van der Pool. The only body I've ever had to carry was being Black in America, man."

"I can't argue with none of that, Tobi. I've been black all day every day. But that's a whole different body and its dead weight, man. It ain't nothing but a heavy load and if you listen to some of the old folks, it ain't as heavy as it used to be. That body might not totally disappear; I don't know. But it don't matter. We been bent, but we ain't never been broken. It's only made us stronger. One day you're a slave, in the morning you're the President. "

"So, how come you ain't running around telling everybody about Jesus Christ and God instead of this poetry shit, van der Pool?"

"I'm called to write poetry which is the same thing as preaching. God's in the poetry, Tobi. And the poetry's in God. You ever read Psalms? The twenty-third psalm? I still can recite that from when I learned it in Sunday school."

"Can't say I ever got around to, van der Pool."

"Can't get no more poetic than that." Alex lifted his eyes and opened his mouth, rolled scripture upon the ceiling:

"The Lord is my Shepherd; I shall not want. He maketh me to lie down in green pastures; He leadeth me beside the still waters. He restoreth my soul; He leadeth me in the paths of righteousness for His name sake. Yea, though I walk through the valley of the shadow of death, I will fear no evil; for thou art with me; thy rod and thy staff they comfort me. Thou preparest a table before me in the presence of mine enemies; thou anointest my head with oil; my cup runneth over. Surely goodness and mercy shall follow me all the days of my life; and I will dwell in the house of the Lord forever."

"I understand exactly why God left me alone. He's from London, England. You hear that accent on them words, man? Don't no niggers on the South Side I know talk like that. They ain't even got no niggers in London. Do they?"

Alex shook his head. "Tobi. I give you all that magnificent language and all you get out of it is something about London? What about 'valley of the shadow of death?' Isn't that beautiful? The whole poem is rich with meaning and metaphor."

"You sure that Shakespeare fellow didn't write that?"

Alex laughed. "Yeah, I'm sure. Those are God's words. He just used somebody else to put 'em on paper. You ain't got to be religious to dig the twenty-third psalm. Hell, you ain't even got to be saved."

"You saved, van der Pool?"

Alex studied the question, watched dust mites dance upon the top of a desk. "I don't know. Sometimes God talk to me just like you talking to me. Other days, He ain't got nothing say. But over the past few months since all this literature has gotten into me, I know I ain't the same. I don't know if I'm saved or not Tobi, but I'm a believer."

"I can dig that, van der Pool. And I can dig what you say about changing. The only thing that ever stays the same is change. I guess how we deal with it is something else. You saying God is a poet?"

"Of course. There's a story in the Bible called the Prodigal Son. He ain't too bad with fiction either."

Alex heard Tobi clear his throat. *"You better look now. The natives are restless."*

When Alex looked across the room everyone had their hands in the air like ten-year-olds trying to get the teacher's attention. He called on Mr. Strother first.

"I heard you reciting the Twenty-Third Psalm. Can we say the Lord's prayer in unison?"

Alex pushed himself up, walked over to where the others sat. "Nah, man. We done recited and prayed all we gonna recite and pray today. Just relax."

Rose Verdell crossed her legs, uncrossed them and crossed them again, then sighed that she was next. "I have to go to the bathroom."

Alex studied the empty pizza box and two cans of soda before her. "You take your medicine?"

"Yes. Yes, I did, thank you. It makes me go to the bathroom quite often."

"I need you to hold that just a little bit longer until I figure that bathroom thing out. OK?"

Alex nodded in Brandon's direction. "What up, Red?"

"I wanna play for my supper."

"What the hell is that, man?"

"I play guitar and harp. Sometimes at the same time. Got one in my pocket." Red pointed to a jacket lying across a desk.

Alex frowned. "You got one in your pocket right now?"

"Yeah, man," Red smiled. "Guitar wouldn't fit."

Alex smiled. "Let me get the harp. You hold tight."

"I'm not feeling well. Feels like I'm going to throw up." Sara's face was flushed at the cheeks. She pressed the back of her hand against her forehead.

"See there, van der Pool. One person got to probably take a dump and the other got to puke. They probably ate the one that was meant for you."

Alex shook his head. "All right, Sara . . . I can't let you leave. But I'll do what I can."

All the time he was talking to Sara, Monte was waving his hand as though he'd just touched a hot stove. Alex preempted his request. "I promise I'm gonna let you use the phone, dog."

"You told me that almost an hour ago, dog. I could've been done used the phone while you over there talkin' to yourself."

"I know what I said," Alex snapped. "I didn't say when and when the time is right, I'll let you and everybody know. And another thing: It ain't none of your goddam business who I talk to. You say one more thing to me and I'm gonna get that phone and put a bullet through it." Alex's words stretched the silence in the room until the air was about to snap. He watched Monte's hand fall into his lap as if it had been pierced by a fatal shot. Monte glared at him with disdain, disgust, disappointment and Alex mirrored his stare.

"That's getting him told, van der Pool. But you might want to go ahead and cap that sonofabitch right now. Playing all that baseball done made him think he's some kind of hero who deserves to be treated like one."

Megan Fly wore a smile as wide as the semi-circle she sat in the middle of. Her mien was palliative for Alex's agitated state. Tranquility flowed from her, washed over him and flooded the entire room. "What do you need, Mrs. Fly?"

"Poetry," Megan folded her hands in front of her. "I want to hear some more of your poetry, Alex. You think that poetry is worth dying for. Right now, it's the only thing keeping us alive. Do you have any more?"

"Yeah. I got poetry. If I ain't got nothing else, I got poetry."

Alex pushed as many desks as he could toward the front of the room until they clanged into one another. He stacked them atop one another to create as much privacy as he could. Afterward, he grabbed a waste can from the corner and placed it behind the partition. "All right, ma'am." Alex nodded towards Mrs. Verdell. "It's the best I can do." He waved her forward with his gun.

"There's a box of Kleenex on the desk."

Mr. Strother stood, grabbed Mrs. Verdell under the arm and pulled her to her feet. Alex could see her pupils dilated with tears as she walked behind the barricade to the makeshift toilet.

Alex stood with his arms folded and back to the partition as if a sentry proscribed to protect the privacy of Mrs. Verdell. When she finished she rejoined the group by claiming her same spot.

"I need to take a leak."

Alex nodded in the direction of the waste can, watched the others and listened to Tennessee Red release a long stream, bringing it to a stop with short quick bursts.

"Merriweather? Where your cell phone?"

Monte raised his head at the sound of his name. "Right there." He pointed to a blue book bag draped over the back of a desk. Alex waited until Red returned, rummaged the book bag and sailed the phone through the air until it dropped into Monte's cupped hands.

Megan Fly's phone vibrated, emitted three shrill rings where Alex left it on the floor. He shifted the gun from one hand to the other, recognized Sheriff Johnsey's number before answering the phone.

"Sheriff Johnsey?"

"Alex?"

"Mama?" Alex's heart jackhammered against his ribcage.

"Hey, baby." Her voice sounded the way it did when he was a kid after he'd scraped a knee, broken a toy or didn't make the football team his freshman year. "What's the matter?"

"You ok, mama? They treating you all right?"

"I'm fine. But you got me worried. You got us all worried. Your sister and dad are here. We're all all right and we want you to be all right too."

Alex circled the room, waved the gun at nothing in particular. He walked over to the window, parted the blinds with his index finger. He looked for his family but found only law enforcement, the press and a group of spectators behind a barricade. "I'm good. I'm as good as I've ever been. I figured out what I want to do with the rest of my life now."

"That's good, baby. But we both know you can't do it from inside that classroom. Where in the world you get a gun?"

Alex laughed. "I can get a gun easier than I can get just about anything else. That's just the way it is. But I ain't sweating' that. I ain't sweatin' nothing, mama. I like it here. The teacher loves poetry as much as I do and she knows what she's talking about. Me and Tobi are fine."

"Alex, baby." His mother's voice dropped as if it were weighted with a stone. "You need to let everybody go and come on out now. Who is Tobi?"

"I love you, Mama. After Daddy left, you and Margaret was all I ever had. I already told her I love her. Did you get the note?"

"Yes. We got the note and we love you too and we want what's best for you and what's best is to let everyone go and come on out, baby."

"Ain't no point in me going to jail. I'd rather die, Mama."

"We ain't talking no jail."

"Lakeview?"

"Yes."

Alex thought about the two months he spent there a year ago and the first time he was there during high school days. He weighed the electric shock treatments against the long walks he used to take around the campus and how lovely the light fell against the buildings in the afternoon. But most of all he remembered how those walks led to a lake on the edge of the property under a canopy of spruce trees and how once seated on a nearby bench, three ducks squatted before him, looked at him as though they wanted to know where he'd been, what he did when he was there and that they were glad he was back. He always brought a few crumbs from the cafeteria to feed his friends and always meant to ask them where they hung out in the winter time. He wasn't the only one who wanted to know.

Alex didn't know if the counselors at Lakeview cared or not, but he figured they listened 'cause that was their job. And when he left, he didn't feel so anxious, so hopeless. It wasn't jail, but if it was anywhere where poetry didn't matter, it may as well have been. As much as he would miss the ducks, he had no desire to return to Lakeview ever again.

"Ok, Mama. Lakeview it is. But this will be my third time. I can't spend my whole life in a mental institution. I've got poems to write."

"You didn't spend your whole life there the first two times, did you? But you have to save your life this time if you're serious about poetry. You coming out, Alex?"

"Yes."

Alex could feel his mother's smile warm against his ear. She praised Jesus in spite of herself. "You coming out now, baby?"

"Not right now, Mama. I ain't read but one of my poems and the teacher's on to me about reading some more. She basically asked me what I'm here for if I ain't gonna read. So, I'll be out in a minute or two."

"Alex." His name issued angry from his mother's lips as if it would reach through the phone and pull his ear until he complied. But instead, it kissed him on the jaw. "Baby, you need to let those people go now and you need to let yourself go too."

"Let myself go, too? Mama. You been writing poetry?"

"No, baby. I've been praying for you and there are only so many prayers I have left. It's up to you to do what's right from this point on."

"All right, Mama." Alex hung up the phone.

"Nothing. No email, no text, no nothing." Alex looked up and saw Monte with his head thrown back. With eyes squeezed tight, he mumbled something towards the ceiling as if he and God had their own private language. He cursed nothing in particular, rested his head in his hands. "I need to get the hell out of Stovall, dog. Y'all need to be seeing me on the cover of *Sports Illustrated* or on *ESPN* about this time next year."

"Man, whether you're in a magazine or on TV, how could anybody ever forget you?"

Alex's question was for everyone else and there were a few chuckles; Monte had head bowed in concentration, fingers engaged in the construction of email.

The phone vibrated before it rang Alex's hand. He glanced at the number, shook his head.

"Mama. I'm doing what's right and when I get through doing it, then I'll come out."

"Alex?"

"Sheriff Johnsey?"

"Yeah, Alex. It's me. Now, Alex." He heard the Sheriff clear his throat. "You promised your mama you'd let everybody go and come on out. I'm all for getting you some help and I think that'll be best for everyone. But I need everyone to come on out single file with their hands atop their head first and then you last. I promise you, you won't get hurt. Alex? You there? I need to know you're there, Alex."

"Failing to fetch me at first keep encouraged/ Missing me one place search another/I stop somewhere waiting for you."

"Alex. What's that all about, son?"

"You tell me, Sheriff. Matter of fact," Alex was grinning like he was keeping a secret from everyone in the whole world, "just tell me who wrote it and I'll come out right now crawling on my hands and knees."

"Alex. We need to talk. This ain't no Daily Double and I ain't no game show host."

"Man, poetry ain't never been no game. It's always been life or death. I just didn't know it. The clock is ticking, Sheriff. Who wrote that?"

Sheriff Johnsey sucked his teeth. "I don't know, son."

"That's ok, Sheriff. I can get you some help. Hold on one second." Alex hit the speaker button, converted the cell phone into a microphone and suspended it in midair. "Mrs. Fly. Tell the Sheriff who wrote that."

Mrs. Fly cupped both hands around her lips. "Uncle Walt!"

Alex laughed as hard as he could, stomped his feet and when he put the phone back to his ear, his speech was slurred by joy. "Uncle Walt!" he howled. "Sheriff? You hear that? She called him 'Uncle Walt.' Goddam, that's good. Sheriff? You still there?"

Sheriff Johnsey waited until Alex's laughter subsided into a snicker.

"I'm still here, son."

"Where's my mama, Sheriff?"

"Your mama's still right here. But, Alex, we need to talk this thing out once and for all, man."

Alex treaded the floor as if it were eggshells. He turned sideways, making himself small at the window, his finger on the trigger, before peeping through blinds.

He recognized his mother immediately in the green cardigan sweater with the ponytail down her back. Salvador with a toothpick in the corner of his mouth and the Kansas City Monarchs jacket open at the neck and his sister Margaret in blue jeans with arms folded across her chest. They stood next to Sheriff Johnsey, the four of them against a backdrop of the sun ablaze in the tops of trees, the afternoon split in half between light and shadow.

"Alex?"

"I ain't gone nowhere."

"Ain't nothing gone nowhere but time. Precious time. And we can't afford to waste any more of that. Remember when I told you the big boys were here?" He lowered his voice. "Well, they're here from Nashville, too. Guys in suits. I think of myself as a hard ass, but I know their asses are set in stone."

"I ain't worried about none of y'all asses. If anybody comes near that door, I'm going to give them another asshole. What time is it, Sheriff?" Alex moved away from the window, pointed the gun at his hostages who reacted with a collective flinch. He stood over them as if about to take aim.

"It's decision time. It's after four o'clock, Alex. I've given you everything you've asked for and you've promised your mama. Now, you need to give us what we've asked for. C'mon, son. No sense in prolonging this thing. It's all over now."

There was a long pause. "All right, Sheriff. It's just about over now." Alex hung up, laid the phone on a desk and extracted more papers from his book bag. He stood flat-footed, square-shouldered. "Mrs. Fly. This is something I wrote not so long ago. It's called 'Keeper of the Key.'" He read to the class:

"Pain is myself silent imprisoned within,
As the door I slam,
Shut.
The door you try to reach me which,
It opens never.
For only the key of trust the key I have,
That you surrender I must to,
So you can enter into my
Fears, doubts, frustrations failures, losses,
Rejection and my despair.
Until then, I lay continue to will
The bricks alienations isolation of and
Until the wall is complete.
I cannot see.
The closed door is,
Shut.
I am the keeper of the key."

"Man, that's some heavy, heavy blues you puttin' down," Red said. "Not the words so much themselves, but the way you arrange them. Just like the other piece. There a little joint on west Baltimore that has an open mic night every Saturday and your poetry is a lot better than some of the stuff I've heard on that stage."

Alex shook his head. "I don't perform poetry. I write it."

"You want to call it that." Alex didn't see Merriweather's lips move, but knew his voice when he spoke or didn't speak.

He laid the poem on a desk. "What'd you say, motherfucker?"

Everyone looked at Merriweather and Merriweather looked back at them, then at Alex.

"What?"

"What the hell you say about my poetry?"

"What? I ain't said nothing about your poetry. I'm typing an email, dog."

"Bullshit. Stand up and take this like a man." Alex cocked the hammer on the .38, aimed it at the open mouth of Merriweather. "Get up! I got your 'you wanna call it that.' I'm gonna put some Amiri Baraka on your ass. Get up!"

"No, No!" Mrs. Verdell was on her feet before the words were out of her mouth, her outstretched hands more plea than protection. "For the love of God . . . don't. Please."

Before Alex knew it, they all sprang from the floor to form a shield around Merriweather, who remained seated. Sara was the first to speak: "Melancholy. Melancholy, Alex. You've not only done a wonderful job capturing it, but the poem also evokes it."

"I think it's commendable that you could put that down on paper," said Mr. Strother. "It takes a lot of guts not only to write that, but to share it with someone else as well. Especially complete strangers." He shook his head, turned down his mouth. "I don't think I could do it."

Mrs. Verdell cleared her throat. "I don't know a lot, but I do know you're a sensitive soul and your writing shows just how deeply you're in touch with your feeling in a world that cares little about such things. The world can be horrible that way sometimes. Your emotions are like raw nerves, young man. That has to hurt when you touch them. And it hurts to watch you touch them."

"Everybody, sit down before I shoot y'all in the ass. Sit down." When everyone returned to their spots on the floor, Alex pointed at Merriweather. "Give me that phone." He took two steps forward, snatched the phone from Merriweather and hurled it towards the wall where it shattered into pieces across the classroom floor.

"Now, how I know y'all not telling me this 'cause I got this goddam gun?" He held the gun up and away from him like it was a venomous snake. "Why everybody want to bullshit me?"

"Alex," Megan Fly called his name as if he were a mile away instead of across the room, "could I see the poem, please? And a pen?"

Alex handed her both. Twenty minutes later she returned the favor. He lodged the pen behind his ear, read his poem silently with some words scratched through, others circled and Megan's notations in the margins. When finished, he lowered the paper and found her anxious eyes upon him.

"Those are your words, Alex," she blurted. "I merely made a suggestion to make the images sharper, add urgency to the language."

Alex perused the page again, nodded. "I like it."

"Can you read it again? Aloud?"

"Pain is the silent prisoner within myself
As I slam the door,
Shut.
The door in which you try to reach me,
But never opens.
For I possess the key, the key of trust,
That I must surrender to you,
So you can walk into my
Fears, doubts, frustrations, failures, losses,
Rejections, my desperation.
Until then, I continue to lay
Bricks of alienation, isolation
Until the wall becomes me.
and I become the wall.
The door is closed,

Locked shut.
I am the keeper of the key."

Alex half-smiled, nodded again. "I like it. But I think I like mine better. Thanks, anyway."

"You're quite welcome. Remember, those were only suggestions. It's not a matter whether you change anything. What's important is that you be receptive to constructive criticism. That's what you came here for, right? It's ok. You'll make a fine poet one day."

Alex could feel the blood rush hot to his cheeks and thought this must be what blushing feels like. He looked away from Megan Fly. "What you say about it, Red?"

Red was shocked to hear his name. "I already told you, bro. Those are some bitchin' lyrics the way you put 'em down."

"Let me hear what you puttin' down. That yours?" Alex searched both pockets, extracted the harmonica from the inside of the jacket, lobbed it to Red.

Red blew into the harp as if he were trying to clear it of dust. He ran his lips from one end to the other in a breathy effort to tune the instrument. "This is for west Tennessee music legend and my hero, John Lee 'Sonny Boy' Williamson." He blew four bars and stopped in the middle of the fifth. "This is the original 'Sonny Boy' Williamson, Sonny Boy number one, not to be confused with 'Sonny Boy' number two, who was from Arkansas and whose real name was Rice Miller, but used the name Sonny Boy Williamson after the real Sonny Boy was killed. Sonny Boy number one was born right down the road in Jackson around 1914 and like I said was killed in Chicago after a gig in 1948. He was robbed walking home, so the story goes. You can't talk about blues harp without . . ."

". . . Red." Alex shook his head. "Just blow that damn thing, man."

"Sorry. 'This is Good Morning Little Schoolgirl.'" He counted off the beat by stomping his foot four times. The melody and harmony from the harmonica rose and fell in half notes and flatted fifths until the walls swelled with syncopation. The floor roiled in rhythm as the beat became infectious, Alex clapping his hands on the two and four. Mr. Strother helped Mrs. Verdell to her feet and they began to dance in circles around one another turning the classroom into a juke joint of higher learning. The only thing missing was sawdust and a bottle of homemade hooch; Sara smiled, Monte grinned and Megan Fly laughed almost as loud as Red played.

When Red finished, Alex, Sara, and Megan applauded their approval and Monte gave him a fist bump. Mr. Stother and Mrs. Verdell stood over him, hands on hips trying to catch their breath, smiling.

"Goddam, Red!" Alex exclaimed. "That was off the freakin' chain, man. You got mad skills, son. Tobi? You like that? Tobi? Where you at?"

Alex glanced around the room and the others did so uncomfortably. "Where you learn how to play like that, Red?"

"Just by listening, bro. I can read enough music to get by. But everything I've learned about playing I picked up by ear." He reached for another bottle of water, swallowed long from it. "I've got a pretty good collection at my house and when I say collection, I'm talking vinyl. Thirty-three and a half long playing records. Liner notes and all. Some are vintage mono recordings, some live and in stereo. Guess I got close to 500 records all over the house that my mom threatens to toss out every other day."

"Sonny Boy number one, huh?"

"Yeah, bro. He's the pied piper of anybody that ever thought about blowing harp. He's influenced somebody whether they knew it or not."

"Hey. I think I brought a blues poem with me. Hold on."

Mr. Strother and Mrs. Verdell sat back down as Alex skipped over to his book bag. He shuffled one poem after another until he found the right one.

"I awoke morning and the
Was night different from the no,
Had breakfast for blues
Knew right would be everything.

BB King around and spinnin' and round
On CD my brand new,
Talkin giving up bout living,
Wrote just that song for me.

My blue soul is black and,
My loaded heart with lead
You remind my photograph
That I would be better off dead.

Beer and stale, warm is flat
Pig feet don't taste right,
I stumble in the sunshine
Since you took away your light.

Looking baby for my,
Looking for a reason to live,
All possessions my worldly
And anything I would give

To get her back

Find out what I did wrong
Cause one baby without my day
Is one day too long.

I awoke morning and the
Was night no different from the.
Had blues for breakfast
And knew right would be everything.

I'm a black man living in America
What else can go wrong?
These blues are the blue, black
And this is my song."

Alex finished the last word and looked up from the page as though he anticipated applause.

"I love the lines: I stumble in the sunshine/since you took away your light, Alex" Megan began. "The tension and contrast makes the imagery unforgettable."

"Alex?" Mr. Strother flicked lint that wasn't there from his pants. "Since you came here for feedback, I'd like to add my two cents worth." The muscle in his jaw twitched. "What I learned about poetry, I've learned it in this class and honestly, while I don't understand everything you just read, I found the last stanza distracting. For me everything that came before it stayed within the context of the poem. It felt like a real blues song. But that last stanza felt unnecessary to me. Am I the only one who feels that way?" He searched the faces of his fellow captives as if they were life preservers.

"I tend to agree," Sara said. "The final stanza seemed more like an afterthought. It's a fine stanza, mind you, but I'm not sure it belongs in this poem."

Mrs. Verdell nodded. "I think there's the solution right there. Let the last stanza be the beginning of a separate poem or part of a new one.

"I don't see a damn thing wrong with the last stanza," Monte erupted. "The last stanza puts a bow on the whole poem. For me, what came before the last stanza wouldn't make sense if wasn't for the last stanza and sense don't none of it make no sense to begin with, I say leave it alone." Monte frowned, thought of something he'd been thinking of. "Yo, dog? "Why you smash my phone like that?"

Alex frowned at Monte, then ignored him. He looked at Mrs. Fly. "What'd you say?"

Megan removed a wayward strand of hair from her eye, sighed as though she had been waiting to speak for months. "I say what I've already said: we can tell you to take it out and we can tell you to leave it in and you can choose to or choose not to. That's one of the beauties of getting feedback on your work. But eventually, you'll know what to leave in or take out when you find your own voice. The way you express yourself with and through the language will be uniquely yours. You'll develop your own style and once you do so, you'll reinvent that style over and over. That's what the great poets do. That's what any great artist does. And there's no magic formula for that. Just read, study and write as much as you can while you can."

Alex allowed the silence to punctuate her statement. "You ever publish, Mrs. Fly?"

"Oh. A couple of obscure journals," she laughed diffidently. "Most of them long defunct by now."

"Mrs. Fly is being modest, Alex," Sara said. "I wouldn't call the Chattahoochee Review obscure or defunct. And," she stated the word as if it were the last conjunctive on earth, "she has a book out as well that was nominated for a major award."

"A book? What's the name of it?"

Megan dismissed the whole thing with the wave of her hand. "That was over five years ago."

"It doesn't matter. What's the name of it?"

"First Light."

"Word. What was the award?"

"I was just nominated. I didn't win."

"It was the Agnes Starrett Lynch Prize," Sara spoke up.

"Wow." Alex was amazed and confused. "So, what are you doing here?"

The question punched Megan Fly in the solar plexus. She was winded not because of the ferocity of Alex's words, but because they caught her with her guard down. She winced, stammered twice, put breath beneath her words. "Poetry's not as romantic as you may think, Alex. Maybe in the days of Shelly and Byron. But today, the majority of poets teach at somebody's school or a college or university. And even then they have to apply for grants, fellowships, awards to supplement that. Only a handful of poets or writers for that matter are fortunate enough to make a living from their writing. A handful may be a stretch; maybe two or three fingers at the most. I'm here because I needed a job and Stovall State offered me one."

Alex looked away, rubbed his chin and frowned. Everyone he knew had either left Stovall or were making plans to do so. Who in hell moved to Stovall? There are colleges and universities all over the country, so why not take your published book and college degree to where they were? It made no sense. But maybe that's what she was planning, had been planning all along. She knew a lot about poetry, but teaching here in Stovall made no sense. Something had to be holding her here. Maybe she was bullshitting him all along. Or maybe she was bullshitting herself. Poets are known for that. The wrinkles in his forehead were part confusion, part disbelief. He looked at Megan Fly and smiled. "OK." He winked at Red. "Hey, Red. Spread some of them goddam blues around."

Red smiled as if he were on stage with lights bright and hot. "All right. This is an original called Blues in B Flat Major." He blew the first few notes and Alex snapped his fingers to the beat, danced his way across the floor into a corner of the room. He squatted down, cut the phone on and checked his messages.

17

Megan Fly checked her watch, looked in the direction of the window. She held her hands in her lap to stop them from shaking. It was five o'clock and the live music in the room sounded the way it did down at Sculley's this time of day when she left her office and stopped by the bar on her way home. Sculley's would be filling with other patrons from other professional walks of life by now and those she didn't know by name, their faces had become familiar. Ginger, the bartender, would always start mixing the vodka and orange juice the moment she walked through the door and by the time she made her way to the bar, a screwdriver would be awaiting her arrival. By five thirty, happy hour would officially be Christened by a bar packed full of patrons with half-priced drinks in hand.

On Tuesday morning, her first class wasn't until 11 am and that meant a lecture on the Harlem Renaissance. It was all part of Advanced Sophomore Lit. Tuesday always afforded her the opportunity to sleep late, read for an hour or so and meditate upon the day's schedule. She had become respected by students and peers, most of them anyway and knew that it was a matter of time before she would be granted tenure status. But Alex's question was a boomerang that returned to her mind no matter how many times she tried to dismiss it. *What are you doing here?* She'd asked herself that question when she first moved to Stovall four years ago and found herself addressing it at least once a year since then. She enjoyed teaching, felt that she was born to do it, but had always envisioned herself teaching at a four-year institution of higher learning, preferably a private college with ivy-covered walls, a prestigious name and alumni endowments. *What are you doing here?* But instead, she had labored for the past three years at a state college, junior college no less, Stovall Community College. But teaching was teaching. Whether you taught at Oxford or in an outhouse, you either loved it or you didn't, did it because it was what you wanted to do. What she didn't love was the boredom of routine. The long drive into work, departmental meetings, grading papers, the long drive home. Thank God for Sculley's. Standing before a classroom of students espousing the virtues of the world's greatest literature produced a euphoria that outweighed any negative connotations. Even if the students looked at her like they didn't know what she was talking about or wondered if she knew what she was talking about, the excitement and passion with which she delivered her commentary could never be questioned. Her students said she made literature come alive. If it was anything she loved more than teaching it was when that light came on in her students' eyes and they too began to share the enthusiasm about great works of literary art or the ideas espoused within it. When the light came on in her Advanced Sophomore Lit class, it illuminated the souls of a cross-section of humanity: unemployed factory workers, housewives, professionals, kids fresh out of high school not knowing what in hell to do with their lives or only vague notions of what life was about.

Megan shifted her attention from the window to Brandon. She encouraged the scraggly, red-headed kid to follow his dreams, even if it carried him into the heart of the Black man's music. She trusted Monte would use his anger as fuel to propel him towards the limitless sky; if not, he would crash and slow burn in Stovall. She envied Sara for the life that she carried in her body, the same life that three miscarriages had taken from her own body. She admired Rose and some days had trouble determining which battle was greatest for her: illness or identity. Mr. Strother, who usually came to class in shirt and tie in preparation for a job when there was no job, she respected. Megan looked at their faces and realized that she loved them all and all those like them that she had taught over the years.

What are you doing here? Who in hell was this kid to ask her a question like that? In one way, in particular, he reminded her of her husband. Yes, the kid obviously had a mental problem, talking to himself, calm one minute, irate the next and no one in his right mind would burst into a classroom and pull a pistol for the love of poetry. But she saw the same passion in his eyes that had possessed her husband.

Five years ago, the University of New Haven an adjunct professorship was here for Megan Fly until her father-in-law bought the farm and her husband, Michael, inherited the 200-acre property. Michael came home from work one Friday evening and announced that he was quitting his job as a law partner of O'Brien, Markson, and White, that they were moving to west Tennessee and that he wanted to paint. She reminded him that she was tenured at the University of New Haven, that she was thinking about writing another book and that that's what artists did today. She admired his passion to pull life up by the roots in search of fields fallow with self-expression and if no such place existed, he would plow a land of his own. She had no problems with that. Artists had done that and will continue to do that. But to do so when you're twenty years of age and single is a lot easier than when you're married and in your mid-forties. She'd told him that it was possible to hold a job and create art at the same time and that it's what she did every day. William Carlos Williams was a physician and a great poet. He could still be a lawyer and an artist as well. When that didn't convince him, she'd thought maybe he'd gotten fired and didn't know how to tell her. That was ok; he could always start his own firm. But after supper, they stayed up well past midnight and the earnestness of his words, sincerity in his eyes convinced her that this was something he had to do. He had to paint and the rural life was an idyllic setting to do so. All this had been pre-ordained, he explained and he was just accepting his destiny. And if he didn't make it as an artist, he would make it the way his daddy did by tending livestock and raising crops. He couldn't he told her, go back to that office or any office and sit behind some desk and pretend to be happy. There was no air to breathe there. If he was not going to do this now, he was never going to do it. He hoped she would understand. Before sunrise, Megan Fly began making plans to contact a realtor to sell their four-bedroom house.

A year later, she choked on the fumes of tractors, sipped sweet tea in the afternoons and swatted mosquitoes thick as the humidity on a summer's night. Stovall State needed an assistant professor and the Fly's needed money. Teaching is teaching. And since his grand announcement, Michael hadn't sold a painting. He'd placed in a couple of local contests, but that hadn't paid any bills. After a year, she'd figured he'd say the hell with it, sell the farm, tell her to pack their belongings for the northeast and go back doing what he'd spent thousands of dollars and countless hours training to be a lawyer. But rejection and disappointment only served to strengthen his resolve and he continued to stalk that dream. He was determined to paint whether anyone bought them or not. Besides, his head of cattle were increasing and so was the price of beef. It wasn't the salary of a law partner, but it didn't cost as much to live here than it did in New Haven and they were doing ok now.

What are you doing here?

Megan began to shake, disguised her tremors by fidgeting. The first shot of vodka and OJ made the world seem lighter, allowed her to shed the day's troubles that clung to her skin. Michael kept telling her that they were all right and he may have been at peace with himself, but nothing had been ok with her for over a year. She missed the laughter of friends at cocktail parties, longed for train rides into the city that disembarked on Broadway, grieved for the beauty of snowfall against the winter of her life. She'd made a handful of friends in Stovall, but after kids, sports and church, their lives left little room for anything much related to anything. Besides, she was still a Yankee and most times when she opened her mouth was jokingly reminded of it. Alex's question wasn't a new one. Megan had long entertained the thought. Last year she asked Michael to consider selling the property so they could move back home. But he'd fallen in love with the smell of dirt, informed her that a gallery in Memphis was interested in a one-man show.

What are you doing here? She thought about Sara's praise for her first book and wanted to tell her, the class or anyone that would listen that she was working on a second collection of poetry. Like salmon spawning upstream, she had to go wherever the language led her and she knew if she didn't follow her instincts and get out of Stovall, with or without Michael, she would drown in the very thing that gave her life. She licked her lips, tried to swallow a cold glass of vodka and orange juice.

16

Alex looked up from his phone at the same time Red was choking the last notes from a ditty. Mr. Strother and Ms. Verdell were doing more talking than dancing, reminiscing about the numerous dance halls that had disappeared around the county.

"Hey, Red," Alex walked across the floor. "Everybody take five." He was about to motion the dancers to take a seat when the phone rang. "Sheriff Johnsey. What's going on?"

"I wish I knew. You tell me what's going on?"

"Aw, man. The joint is jumping."

"All right, Alex. These games are starting to wear thin, man. If you don't tell me what you want I'll have to figure it out on my own. And I don't think that's still necessary. I know you're tired. I know everyone's tired. God knows I am. It's evening now . . . "

". . . Man, it's been evening all afternoon."

"Ok . . . Just send everyone out single file, Alex. You've gotten everything you've asked for. Just come out with your hands above your head and we all go home. Ok?"

"I'm just glad it's not snowing, Sheriff. You? Home, you say?" Alex whipped the pistol from his waistband, made his way over to the window. The sun had fallen into the earth and in its place had risen the glare of lights, cameras and the hum of machines, men. From his vantage point, it appeared the whole world had gathered outside a college classroom in Stovall, Tennessee, on a Tuesday evening. A handful of cops morphed into the National Guard, talking heads were providing expert analysis from their news desks with instant replay and bystanders had blossomed into gawkers, thrill seekers, and protestors. If nothing else, Alex thought, they looked like they were having a good time. He imagined cotton candy being licked from fingers, a bottle of something being passed around and at any moment a Ferris wheel would come tumbling out of the night sky. And the longer he looked the more the scene swelled, throbbed an inch at a time devouring all in its path, increasing in height and girth towards the classroom building and his portal upon the world. So this is the way it was going down? He had turned into the main attraction at the county fair. The freak show to end all freak shows. And the crowd could never get enough, would never do so. Only blood, his blood, would satisfy their lust. It was him against the world. He realized he couldn't win; no one ever did. He just wanted to be remembered for a few lines of poetry.

Alex blinked, rubbed his eyes. "Tell you what, Sheriff. Let me get some trash bags and some more bottled water."

"Trash bags?"

"Yeah. I need to flush the waste basket."

Alex took one last look out of the window, knew that there was nothing he could do to stop the world from moving, that he had set an avalanche of events into motion and it was nothing he could do to get out of the way. He hung up the phone, thrust the gun back into his waistband. "Here," he handed the phone to Megan Fly. "Take this damn thing. I don't need it any-more, but you do. Matter of fact, I want everybody to get up one at a time and get your cell phones and call somebody you know or somebody you don't know and tell 'em you love 'em. This is it."

"Alex."

He ignored Mrs. Fly, nodded at Sara to go first. Monte was about to open his mouth, but Alex held up his hand and stopped his complaint before it could spill from his lips. "Use somebody else's." When everyone had retrieved their phones, Alex stomped to a corner in the room.

"Alex? What about the poetry?"

"Not now, Mrs. Fly." He squatted, buried his head in his hands. Alex heard a noise beyond the door, the movement of footfalls fading. He jerked to attention, the hairs on his forearms standing on end, underarms producing rings of sweat. "Tobi? Tobi. That you?"

"Yeah, van der Pool. It's me."

"Man, where you been? Thought you'd run out."

"You should know better than that, van der Pool. I been done running for a while. Tell you where I have been, though: I was sleep until that white boy started playing that harp."

"What'd you think about that?"

"He can sing and blow. I'm going to have to rethink what I said about white folks and the blues. He's ok. Matter of fact this whole thing right here is ok, van der Pool."

"What whole thing, Tobi?"

"This crime here. Hostage situation. Yep. It's a lot more crimes a nigger can get involved with today than in my day. Used to be a time when all we did was steal hubcaps or rob a corner store. But nothing like this. This bold shit, van der Pool. It takes guts to pull something like this off. They might can say a lot of things about you, but one thing they can't say is that you scared. Yeah. A nigger today got options when it comes to crime: he can sell narcotics, rob banks or rob cars while people still in them. Hell, he can even ride in a car, roll down the window and start shooting at other niggers for no reason at all."

"Tobi?" Alex wiped his hands on his pants.
"Yeah?"

"I been meaning to ask you, what kind of name is that?"

"What kind of name is what? My name?" Alex heard Tobi laugh and it throbbed against his right temple. *"Man, Tobi is an African name."*

"I thought that was a slave name that they had to beat out of a Mandingo warrior. You that same guy?"

"You got the wrong Tobi, van der Pool. I can't be broken and I got both my feet intact. I'm a world traveler, man. You think yours is the first imagination I've ever visited? Think twice. That Hughes fellow might've known rivers, but I've known writers, musicians and artists. But I'm counting on you this time, van der Pool. If you make it, then I'll be famous. Or infamous. Just as long as they spell the name right, goddammit. That's Tobi with an I. One day, ain't no words on a page in a book will be able to hold me down. Or back. I'm going down as one of the best in the world. You wait and see. I'm gonna hang out with Holden Caulfield, Jay Gatsby, Madame Bovary, Lolita, Stephen Dedalus, Gregor Samsa, Mrs. Ramsay and a whole bunch of more folk who were born in a book and refused to ever die. How you gonna know them and not know me? You'll find out. Hell, if I ever catch up with Tarzan, I'm going to kick his ass. Man, with your help, I plan on changing history. And I will. The universe will be too small to hold my name. That's the kind of name I got . . . Now, I've heard of a swimming pool and a cesspool, but what the hell is a van der Pool?"

Until now, Tobi had pronounced his name hundreds of times. But this time it was different. His name traveled a great distance and landed against his ear hollow and detached like an echo or a kite with a severed string against the blue sky. He flipped the question over and over in his mind and each time he did he could not find an answer beneath it. Alex didn't know what kind of name van der Pool was, where it came from and very little about the person who gave it to him.

"My old man . . ." Alex broke off, his eyes clouded with longing.

"What about your old man? He a white dude?"

"Naw. He's Black. . .Some white folks adopted his grandfather, though . . . That's how he got the name van der Pool . . . He cut out on me, on us when I was eight . . . That's about all I know about Scot van der Pool."

"I grew up without an old man, too. Got killed working on the railroad or something. That's what the kinfolk always said. Don't think it was Tennessee, though. But look, man, forget about him and all that. You owe me, remember? You were going to tell me about some lesser charges somewhere in Shelby County."

Alex dropped his head back into his hands, rubbed it as if there were a Genie inside who would appear and explain everything. He was silent a long time before he spoke. "Tobi . . . you ever loved a woman?"

Tobi wrestled with the question until he had it under submission. *"I can't say that I have, van der Pool. It takes so much to live in this stinking world, by the time you give all that you have just to make it from day to day, there ain't enough of you left to give to nobody else. At least it wasn't for me anyway . . . Can't say I ever loved a woman. But I loved being with them. Loved a couple of 'em to death."*

Alex looked up again, his mouth open in astonishment. "You've killed somebody?"

"No. I've did in a couple people. Both of 'em women. One black and one white. Woulda smoked a couple more folks that rubbed me the wrong way, but they was lucky and got away."

"What happened? With the women, I mean?"

"That's one of the things I like about you, van der Pool. You always pushing and probing and wanting to know too damn much. I'll tell you this much: one night I was cleaning my gun, one like the one you got there and it went off and killed the black girl. Her name was Dorothy. The white girl her name was Dianne. I just choked the shit outta her."

"That's cold, man. How you get away with that, Tobi?"

"Dianne? They still looking for the body." Alex heard Tobi laugh, then become serious. *Dianne and I were killing each other gently from the day we met. She wouldn't come around my folk, I was afraid to go around hers. We was always peeping and hiding, slipping and sliding. And when we were out together, like a movie or dinner or some shit like that, the stares and whispers and sometimes the outright insults were just like somebody taking a knife and castrating me. She felt just as bad. One of us was bound to wind up dead sooner or later."*

"I don't know, Tobi. There's a lot more mixed couples now living their lives and not caring who cares about it."

"Yeah. I saw some of them on my way over here and I couldn't help but to be shocked. I say more power to them. But you know and I know that they better know where to go and where not to go. As long as they live in America, believe me, they better care."

"They say in a few years, white folks will be a minority in this country. I don't know if that'll make things better or not. I just think when it comes to somebody you want to be with, either you dig that person or you don't. Whose fucking business is it anyway? Race shouldn't have a damn thing to do with that."

"I'm not arguing with you, van der Pool. I agree. You can be with who you want to be with. Ain't no difference between white women and black women. I anybody should know, it would be me."

Alex laughed out loud, shook his head. "Tobi. Man, you something else. How come you ain't got no last name?"

Alex watched Tobi shake his head. *"The same reason Elvis, Oprah and Prince don't. It ain't even necessary, man . . . Now, Shelby County, van der Pool. Shelby County."*

Alex quieted and looked at the five hostages, four on their phones. He focused on a spot above their heads and let memory ascend the wall until it lifted him from the classroom beyond Dyer Hall and into the back then.

Back then, Alex poured out his life in twelve-hour shifts. Every morning, five days a week, he rose at six, was out of the house and at the offices of Mid-South Distributors by seven. He collected his orders for the day, climbed into a truck and moved through the streets of Memphis making stops to deliver beer along the way. There was freedom in the structure of routine. He, Alexander van der Pool, donned a uniform and commanded tons of steel around the city. Every day he fastened himself into the cab of his truck and every day he was in charge of something, if only for a half day. For those hours of the day, he determined who received beverages and who didn't. And he was good at what he did and knew it. Through drought or storm, he never failed to deliver on time. It had become habit for him to be greeted with freebies from restaurant managers and store owners alike whom he knew on a first-name basis. His days were planned out weeks in advance and as long as he took his medication, the world always stayed balanced. Driving not only empowered him, but there was nothing like feeling the sun and wind against his skin.

Alex drove a truck for seven years and had received raises each year. He was taking his meds regularly and making enough money and moved out on his own after a year on the job. Mom was right across town and that was a good thing as far as Sunday dinners were concerned. Mid-South Distributors had wanted to promote him to supervisor last year, but he just couldn't see himself exchanging the freedom that the road provided for a suit and tie behind an office desk. But he understood that it was inevitable. He gave Mid-South Distributors everything he had for eight hours a day and they provided him with money, health insurance, and the confidence to be a man.

When he finished his final delivery he could find no complaint with the world. Not only because he'd done what he was supposed to do the way he was supposed to do it, but because Caroline was waiting at the end of those twelve hours. They'd met when he'd made a delivery at the Half Shell on Poplar Avenue where she was a waitress.

From the right side of the room, she moved towards him and brought the whole world with her in slow motion. All Alex saw was long black hair, hazel eyes on a petite brown frame across his peripheral vision and the closer she got, the anticipation of her presence grew. Like when he was a kid at the county fair and he gasped when the rollercoaster fell from its peak. While he waited for the manager to emerge from his office, she smiled at Alex and he could feel the warmth of it rise over his face. After unloading twenty-five cases of beer, Alex pulled the truck off the parking lot and was two miles away when he doubled back and returned to the restaurant. He told the manager that he'd left a pair of gloves behind, but went looking for that fine brown dream instead. He found her, introduced himself. Her name was Caroline. Caroline Spencer.

Over a period of weeks, phone calls became dinners and movies, walks to nowhere. He'd had girlfriends before, but there was a part of himself that he never allowed anyone access to, a place where no amount of hurt could ever reach. But with Caroline, he felt the way he'd never felt about any woman before. As with any female, he was attracted to her physically. Who wouldn't be; she was breathtaking. But he just didn't want sex. He wanted her to know his frailties, faults and when he confessed his battles with schizophrenia over the past five years she accepted his vulnerabilities, told him that they were the things that made him who he was and to not change a thing. He had found someone with whom he could just be himself, someone he could build a life with.

They didn't sleep together until four months later during a weekend getaway to Hot Springs. Alex never forgave the sun for pulling back a corner of the morning, peering through hotel curtains upon their night of lovemaking. It had ended all too soon. Her lips marveling at his chest, arms, thighs. His hands trembling over her breasts, stomach, buttocks. Their gaze poured into the mirror of one another's soul that allowed them to see how they looked in each other's eyes. They only emerged outside of the room's four walls for food, air. Very little changed after their return home to Memphis. The phone calls, texts messages multiplied and they stayed at each other's apartment so often that the inevitable was obvious. His place was bigger and a month later, she moved in with him.

A month after that, Alex thought that he'd been duped by love, felt as though he'd been the victim of an Eros Ponzi scheme or that cupid was a confidence man on a corner who had shown him one thing but had taken him for all he was worth in a game of Three Card Monte. When they were living separately, Alex thought that Caroline would be the one he'd want to spend tomorrow with. But from the moment she unpacked her last bag, she changed and things changed with her. His apartment was to be their apartment, but she treated it like it was hers alone. He didn't mind her changing and rearranging, but to come home every other day to find something where it hadn't been or to have to search for something where it used to be without his consent, pissed him off for days. But he was willing to forgive and he did.

One Friday in mid-August was a hell of a day. It was 90 degrees at nine a.m. when the air conditioner in the truck went out and by three o'clock it was well over 100 when the truck went out altogether. By the time the mechanic got to him and got him going three hours later, Alex still had four stops to make. Two of his customers understood that some things couldn't be helped, one cursed him under his breath and the other never made eye contact with him or had anything to say at all. Of all the responses, the last one was the worst. He would have preferred to be called the vilest name on the planet than to be treated as if he never existed in the world or never would. This was the first time that Alex was not where he was supposed to be on time. When he pulled his Ford-150 into the parking lot of his apartment complex at the end of the day, he killed the engine, sat behind the wheel staring into nothingness vast and precipitous. He exited the pickup and hoisted the world upon his shoulders, dragged his feet towards his front door one numbed step at a time. When he turned the key in the lock, it was 7:30. Caroline met him at the door.

"Hey, baby. What in the world happened?" She was barefoot in blue short shorts and a white t-shirt. Supper was on the stove, plates on the dining room table. She pecked him on the jaw.

"Life."

Caroline draped her arms around his neck. "It's all right. Mama'll make it better." She kissed him on the lips. "You get cleaned up. I'll get dinner."

In the shower, Alex flipped on the hot water, let it cascade down upon him like the day's events. He replayed conversations, rearranged images, reconsidered what he would have done differently or let remain the same. And out of his recollections arose a revelation like steam fogging up the bathroom mirror: it was only 7:30. He exited the bathroom in bathrobe and slippers, was drying his hair with a towel when he walked into the kitchen.

"What happened to you? Slow night?"

"What'd you mean?"

"The restaurant closes at eleven. It's not quite eight o'clock." His face was an open question waiting for her to fill in the blank.

"That's what I want to talk to you about."

They had pork chops and mashed potatoes for dinner and afterward, moved to the couch for a glass of wine. She sipped her drink, fingered the rim of the glass. "I'm going to quit my job. I'm applying for an associate degree to be a dental hygienist."

Alex draped the towel around his neck, drank from his glass with one long swallow. "You've already stopped working?"

"Not yet. But when I'm accepted, I'll have to. It's a one-year intensive program and there won't be time for anything else but study."

Alex swirled her words around with what remained in the bottom of his glass. "How you gonna pay for all this? School ain't cheap. Nothing's cheap" He poured himself another drink.

"I'll get loans, like everybody else," she assured him. "But what I don't get, I may need your help."

"Uh-huh," he grunted, adjusted the towel around his neck. "You know this will put us in a tight spot for a while, right?"

Caroline set her glass upon the table in front of them. "I understand. But if we're going to be together, I don't want to be scraping by on waitress's tips. We're going to need some real money. Dental hygienists make about fifty a year, if not more. With that, we can start thinking about moving out of this apartment to somewhere better. I'm not getting any younger. We're not getting any younger. I have to make this move right now. I would rather be in a tight spot for a little while than be stuck in one for the rest of my life." She picked up her glass, finished the wine. "We are going to be together, aren't we?"

Alex looked into her eyes. In them, was her persistence to have the last word and the battles it caused when he refused to surrender it to her, the financial difficulties that would arise when there would be not enough money to cover the days in the month and her rising jealousy that always accused him of lusting after women he stared at or casually glanced at those he'd never seen before. And the deeper he looked the more he longed for just a flash of hope that everything would be all right, would work out in the end, that they would be married and he'd have a son to carry his name. Alex took one last look, searched for the Caroline of his first love, found instead enough faith in the both of them until the light would come along.

"Of course we are." He grabbed her by the nape of the neck, pulled her towards him until he felt the softness of her lips press against his.

Two months later, she was accepted into a dental hygienist program and was to start in the fall. As Alex rounded Alabama Avenue onto Jones Street after an eight-hour shift on a Tuesday evening, he wondered what Caroline had simmering on the stove. As insecure and jealous as she could be sometimes, that never interfered with her cooking. She was equally adept at baking, boiling or frying and one of the best things about coming home was what he would find on the table. Instead, when he removed his key from the lock and stepped inside the apartment, nothing assailed his sense of smell. He checked his watch, noticed two boxes beside the door. He craned his neck, peered closer and noticed the boxes contained clothing, his clothing.

"Caroline!" He took a double take, frowned.

He called to her a second time and the only answer was the thud of things being thrown around randomly and rapidly from their bedroom. A rush of adrenalin sent waves of electricity through his body, threw his heart off rhythm and caused his mouth to go dry. He kept his .38 in the bedside table and from the way it sounded, he would have to wrestle with whoever was ransacking the place to get to it. He called for Caroline a second time, grabbed a brass statue by the neck from a table in the foyer and prepared for battle

He loosened the grip on his weapon when he met Caroline halfway down the hallway. "Hey. What's going on? You all right?"

"No. I'm not all right. I've got herpes." She put her hands on her hip daring him to advance or retreat.

Alex dropped the statue, the hardwood flooring echoed its fall. "What the fuck you talking 'bout, Caroline?"

"I had to get a physical for school next month and I tested positive for Herpes II. What do you have to say about that, Alex?" She pointed her finger at his nose.

"I ain't got shit to say about that. You didn't get it from me." He shook his head, smiled.

Caroline took one step closer towards him. "Oh. You think it's funny, huh? I know you've been cheating. You're always flirting with somebody right in front of me and then deny it when I call you on it. So, why would I think you wouldn't deny this?

"I don't know what you think and right now, I don't care. You didn't get it from me."

"You're the only person I've been with."

"Can't help it. What about the person you were with before me? Or the person you've been with since you've been with me? I got my own reasons to be suspicious. You damn near sleep with that cell phone."

Her nostrils flared. "You bastard!" She shoved him in the chest, caused Alex to lose his balance. She marched back to the bedroom and returned with another box. "Get out!" Caroline thrust the box against Alex's mid-section. His eyes fluttered from the steely glare of her own, landed upon the box in front of him. He didn't know whether to scream or cry, instead uttered something in between and fell to his knees. Atop his socks and underwear, his father stared at him from a photo torn in half. He wanted to speak, wanted to tell her or anyone who would listen that this was the only picture of his father he'd ever owned, that ever since he was eight years old he'd talked to this picture every night before going to bed, that the older he gotten the more he saw his eyes, lips and smiled reflected in that photograph. But instead, Alex held what remained of the picture in both hands, tried to make the two halves snap into a whole. He looked up at Caroline, could only make out the outline of her face through the color red rising up in him with such speed and intensity, he thought the walls of the house were about to explode.

Alex crumbled the photograph, kicked the box down the hall and sprang from the floor. "You bitch." His voice was cool and calculated. His hands were hot and impulsive around Caroline's throat and the harder he squeezed the redder the world became. Even her screams were crimson. She tried to claw and bite her way out of his grip and when that failed, kneed him in the groin instead. Alex disintegrated where he stood, groveled in the hallway until he rolled on his side, heard Caroline's coughs and cries die in the distance.

By the time he struggled to his feet, the echo of the front door slamming still reverberated throughout the house. He squeezed between his legs, sighed when he found two balls still there and wiped tears from his eye.

He limped to his truck, backed out of the driveway and drove south. Twilight had fallen like a thick velvet curtain. And the more he thought about his father's picture shredded in his hallway, the redder the dusk became. Caroline just didn't rip a photograph, she destroyed a part of him that belonged to his dad walking through the front door to be his dad again and Alex would embrace him as the son he was all those years ago.

On Morning Vista Drive, Alex looked left, right, squinted into a sun dying over the western sky. He followed its trajectory, felt his thoughts tumble over the horizon of memory and roll into the lush valley of childhood.

They were going fishing. His father was going to teach him how to grab a writhing worm, bait a metal hook and cast a nylon line. From the river's bank, he was going to get the biggest catfish in the water. He knew Mama would fry it brown and crispy and be proud of him. And his daddy, too. Proud like the time his dad took the training wheels off his bike and ran behind Alex holding onto the seat until he balanced himself before letting go and when Alex was coasting down the street, he looked over his shoulder and saw his dad out of breath, but smiling. Or the Sundays after church and before supper, when they were in the back yard and Alex didn't drop the ball anymore, but retrieved it out of his glove each time and threw a strike back to his dad who smiled and told him how strong his arm was. Or some evenings after he and his dad had stuffed themselves on burgers, fries, Nehi sodas and Moon Pies, they'd staggered to the couch and the last thing Alex remembered was the smile on his father's face as they fell asleep in each other's arm before Mama came home to wake them both.

He had dreamed about it for days, dreamed the same dream. His toes dug into the mud and the more he pulled, the more truculent the catfish became and just as he was about to be pulled into the muddy water, the best part of the dream happened. Alex's became like a tree by the side of the river, muscular and immovable. He didn't know where all his strength was coming from, but he had that catfish on the run at the end of his line. It didn't even feel like he was fishing at all and when he looked up, found his dad over his shoulder, smiling, helping him to reel him in.

When the sun caught up with Saturday morning, it found eight-year-old Alex at six a.m. dangling Jordan's sneakers from aside the bed. He was fully dressed in blue jeans, green shirt, fishing jacket and ball cap. His own tackle box and pole rested at the foot of the bed. The longer he had stayed in bed, the more the sheets seemed to crawl with ants. He and his dad were to eat breakfast at seven, then head to the river; he had been up since four-thirty.

At seven o'clock, he slid his feet under the kitchen table, felt his mother's warm kiss and the wet impression it left on his jaw. The aroma of country ham, toast, grits, and coffee wafted under his nose. He looked up at his mom.

"He went to get the eggs," she responded to the question in his eyes. "That was an hour ago. Let's eat.

No use letting food get cold. We can do without." She sat beside her son, clasped his hand in hers, closed her eyes and gave thanks. After breakfast, she instructed Alex to wait in the other room until his father returned.

He sat on the living room floor in front of the TV with chin resting in his hand and watched Elmer Fudd shoot down a hole at Bugs Bunny, Wiley Coyote blow himself up in pursuit of the Roadrunner and Popeye the Sailor man devour a whole can of spinach with one gulp. He was ten minutes into The Flintstones when he noticed the clock above his head. He got up and cut the TV off, the clock's mechanical ticking counting off the distance to his bedroom. It was nine o'clock.

In his room, Alex closed the door to silence the sound of the metronome on the wall and in his head. In its place rose the voices of his mom and dad arguing late into the night that usually ended with his dad shouting something before the door slammed. Or the promises of his dad that sometimes never caught up with his actions: a Nintendo, the Cub Scouts, a trip to Disney. He listened to the sobs of his mother after his father had been gone for days at a time. After two weeks had passed, she refused to mourn anymore.

Alex nodded off and when he awoke it was past noon. He removed his cap and jacket and went outside to play. He knew the guys would be down the street in the vacant lot by now and would soon be choosing sides for a game of football.

Alex came upon a stop sign before he knew it and skidded to a halt. He realized that he was on Elmore and not really sure how he had gotten there. He turned onto Whitten Road and guessed that this was the way Caroline had gone and when he spotted her Honda just past the I-40 interchange, he gunned his engine towards her rear bumper. He saw that she recognized him in her rearview and the more he honked his horn, flashed his lights, the more she zigzagged through and around traffic. He countered her every move as if the road were a chessboard, tailgated so closely that some drivers thought he was being towed, others that his truck was a shadow of the Japanese import.

He eased off the accelerator, watched her taillights diminish into the distance before him and as he did the torn photo of his father flashed before his eyes and exploded the night into brilliant flame. He stomped the accelerator, pulled behind Caroline in the right lane before ramming the back of her car and watched her sail through the air over the road and into a ditch.

"They charged you with what?" Tobi's voice jerked Alex out of the past, over the wall of memory, dropped him feet first back into the moment.

Alex mused at the idea of his being locked up for a week, his court-appointed attorney, making bail on the condition that he do a second stint at Lakeview. Upon his release, his mother, and the judge agreed that bucolic Stovall was better than urban Memphis and two months later he was sleeping in his sister's spare bedroom. He entertained the idea of revisiting that whole ordeal, but shook his head to rid himself of the notion. None of that mattered now anyway. "It was attempted first degree. But was reduced to especially aggravated assault."

"Sounds like it should've been self-defense to me, van der Pool," Tobi said. *"With all the shit she put you through, sounds like she was trying to do you in."*

"She got banged up pretty good. But feels like I got the worst of it . . . I admit what I did was wrong. I just lost it and when I did I lost everything. Job, money, crib. Last I heard, she was on the mend and was getting on with her life. I got my sister's bedroom and Stovall."

"You still love her don't you, van der Pool?"

"I used to tell myself I didn't. But she hurt me bad, man. Real bad. This wound right here might heal sooner or later," he fingered the spot about his right eye. "But the one she gave me might not ever stop bleeding."

"Were you cheating?"

"Naw, man. Later found out that the test was a false positive. A motherfucking false positive. Can you believe that? All that for nothing." Laughter came short and bitter. "But if I could change things, I don't know if I would or not. Without my sister's bedroom and being back in Stovall, there would be no poetry. You understand what I'm saying, Tobi? Without poetry, there would be no me. It's all I got, man."

"What did your old man say about not making that fishing trip?"

"Nothing. I never saw him again. After that it was just me, Margaret and Mama. And like Mama said, we did without. Eggs ain't everything. But I always expected that man would come back one day. Mama did too.

That's why she didn't re-marry for a long time, I guess."
As soon as he finished his words, the light from another thought rose over his mind: he wondered if his dad ever thought about him. Did his dad ever think about him learning how to pull a necktie into a knot, prepare hot lather for a sharp razor, drive a stick shift or who had served his country in war, sat behind a desk in his own office or had become a man in the image of his old man who had grandkids in the world somewhere.

"I don't know, Tobi. Maybe I need to thank Caroline."

"What's that?"

"She gave me one less lie to believe in."

"Whatever you say, van der Pool. But I say that chick gave you the blues, man. A sudden case of food poisoning or a fall down a flight of stairs would have done her some good."

Tobi's voice dissipated as those of Alex's captives became a cacophony of chatter on their phones.

"Go ahead and send me the admission papers. I'm going to enroll at UT in the fall," Rose Verdell instructed her daughter. "And Linda, check with the Financial Aid Office. I should qualify for that."

"Oh, Mama. You don't have to worry about any tuition. We told you we would take care of that. I just wish you would've come up here this fall. All of this could've been avoided, at least for you anyway . . . how do you feel? You being treated ok?"

"I had a sick spell earlier, but I'm much better now," Rose said.

"That bastard wouldn't let you go even though you're taking chemo? You able to take your medicine?"

"No. Yes. But that's all right. He's a lot more sick than I am. At least, I've been able to get some help."

"Has he tried anything with you, mama?"

Rose laughed. "No. He's been very respectful. Besides, who wants a woman going through menopause and cancer?"

"You'd be surprised. It's all over the news that he's crazy and violent and has a long police record."

"Well . . . I don't know about that." She lowered her voice as if putting her hand over the mouthpiece. "He's moody and he's looking at me right now. So I don't want to get into any of that." She perked up again. "Where's my baby?"

"Hold on."

"Hey, Nana!" It was Rose's nine-year-old granddaughter.

The first time Rose heard that word she wondered about its origin and when and where did grandkids all over the country have a convention to vote out the word *grandmother* and elect *nana* instead. But now she appreciated how youngish, hip and colorful it sounded on the lips of her nine grandchildren, how warm it felt against her ear. "Hello, Hannah. How is my darling pumpkin?" Hannah, the youngest of Linda's three children, wore her hair in two brunette pigtails.

"I'm doing fine."

"School all right?"

"Yes."

"You being nice to your brothers?"

"Yes. We were all watching you on TV, Nana. Mama and Daddy too."

"Is that so?"

"Yes. We're on our way to watch you in person now."

Rose hesitated. "What?"

Hannah couldn't contain her glee. "We got out of school early. We're on our way to Stovall in the middle of the week, Nana!"

"Let me speak to your mother, pumpkin."

"We're about an hour away, Mama," Linda's voice traveled as though she were talking long before she put the phone to her mouth. She anticipated her mother's objections and pre-empted them. "I know, I know. It's nothing we could do in Stovall, but it's nothing we can do in Knoxville either, so if we're going do nothing we may as well do it as a family with you. We just couldn't sit at home. Watching everything on TV was making us crazy. One minute they're saying this, the other that. We had to do something. Everybody's on the way to Stovall, Mama. Me, Adam and Frank are driving; Cynthia and Jake are on airplanes."

"Goodness." Rose felt tears welling in her throat, dabbed the corner of her eye to keep them from spilling. "Did the kids get anything to eat before you left?" She could hear exasperation mounting in her daughter.

"Yes, Mother. We left a drive thru not long ago."

"A drive-thru? Linda, those kids need fruits, vegetables, and lots of water. And so do you and Ted. Do you know what's even in that drive thru stuff? Chicken nuggets. The way they shoot steroids into everything nowadays, chickens are probably growing nuggets and God knows what else. All that processed food does is cause sickness and obesity. I can witness about the sickness part. As far as the obesity goes . . . is it any wonder that the diabetes rate among our kids continues to climb . . ."

"Mama? That's one of the main reasons we're coming down there so you can cook us one of those Sunday dinners like you used to when we were growing up. Cynthia and I can help, like we used to. You remember?"

"Of course, I do. That's a wonderful idea. No point in waiting for Thanksgiving or Christmas. We need to get together just because we can. And that'll be a good time to figure out what I need to do with the house before the fall."

"We love you, Mama."

"I love you all, too. We'll have banana pudding for dessert."

"Man, I can't wait to get down there." If Monte could have jumped through the cell phone, he would've hugged the Florida State University coach on the other end. "I've been checking my email and phone calls all day and when I didn't hear anything, I thought you guys had changed your mind."

"No, we hadn't changed our mind, Monte," the Coach's voice boomed. "We left messages at your home this morning. But once we learned about what was going on, your safety took precedence over everything else. The scholarship is yours if you still want it." The coach paused. "Are you ok?"

Monte could hear the frown in the coach's voice. "I was doing good. But now after talking to you, man, I'm doing great! I'm just ready to get down to Tallahassee."

"I've been trying to follow events as close as I could. When did you get released? Everybody get out ok?"

"We ain't out yet," Monte laughed.

"Where are you calling me from?"

"I'm at Stovall State."

"You're still in the classroom, son?"

"Man, I been a hostage all day."

Monte heard the Coach swallow. "Monte . . . I think we need to get off. I don't know if the police would want you talking to anybody on the outside right now and it's no point in aggravating that guy anymore than you need to."

Monte laughed again, but this time not so loudly. "He was the one who told me to use the phone. Actually, it's the teacher's phone and I need to hand it back in a minute." He turned his head to the side to lower his voice. "The bastard smashed mine up against a wall. He ain't playing with nine men on the field and the ones he got keep chasing pitches out the strike zone. I don't know what the police know. I don't even know where the hell they at, but I wish someone would tell them it's the bottom of the ninth. I just hope this game's over soon, coach, so I can pack my bags and get out of here. I'll be the best center fielder you've ever had."

"If the guy is as unstable as you say he is, then we better cut this short. But before we do, you need to know this: Jerry Hernandez will be transferring from Arizona State this fall and he's going to be starting in centerfield. You familiar with Hernandez?"

Monte's stomach turned two and a half somersaults, left the taste of bile on his tongue. "Yeah, I know Hernandez. Thought he went in the first round to the Mets? What the hell he doing in Florida?"

"He went number three in the first round, but he wants to be the first in his family to graduate college and just so happens most of his family now lives in Florida. I don't need a centerfielder, Monte, but first base is wide open. What'd you say?"

Monte flipped the question over in his mind, hoping to find an answer beneath it. Ever since he was eight, baseball was all he'd ever known. From Little League to Dizzy Dean to High School and now junior college, it had always been the sound of a ball flying off a bat, the smell of well-worn leather gloves and grass stains on the seat of his pants. He thought football barbaric and basketball all right. But baseball was the game of heroes. Heroes that became legends, legends into mythic figures. Babe Ruth, Jackie Robinson and his favorite of all time, Say Hey, Willie Mays. If anyone ever wanted to know anything about Monte Merriweather he's always said, don't go looking for his birth certificate, just do a reference check or search his academic transcript. All you had to do was look at all his scorecards. They would swear to his courage for all the times he stole third, testify to his unselfishness when he sacrificed himself to advance the runner and evince his ability to adapt to change each time he lined a base hit to the opposite field. His world had always revolved around centerfield, but now the planet was shifting, leaning towards a Hispanic who was bigger, stronger, had two good knees and a professional contract when he wanted it. But baseball is baseball, he reasoned. You have to run, hit and catch whether you're eight or thirty-eight, whether you're climbing the wall chasing homers or pulling grounders from the dirt. He simply would have to do what he had to do. If there were no first base, that would only leave Stovall and he would have to charge this fool with a gun and force him to pull the trigger.

"I'll give it a shot, coach. I just want to play." He could almost hear the coach's face stretch into a smile.

"That's the right attitude, Monte. And that's not to say you won't see some time in centerfield, you just won't start there. You'll be a great asset to our team and we think we can help develop your game. We're really proud of the way you've rehabbed the knee and improved academically as well. We're expecting big things from you."

"Coach?"

"Yeah, Monte?"

"Number 25 is the only number I've ever worn . . . "Monte trailed off into insinuation.

"Twenty-five, huh? Tell you what," Coach cleared his voice. "When all this blows over, a couple of coaches and I will come up to the campus and do an official press conference and have you signed on the dotted line. It'll be a national event. We'll bring a number 25 jersey with your name on it. How does that sound, champ?"

"Sounds like a dream I've been trying to have all my life."

"All right, Monte. We need to get off this phone and when we hang up. I don't want you to do nothing stupid and try to be some kind of hero. Just let the authorities do their jobs and you get out of there safe and sound. OK?"

"All right, Coach," Monte whispered. "I'll see you later."

"I'll see you first, twenty-five."

"Mom. I've made up my mind, made it up a long time ago," Red explained. "This is what I need to do."

"But it's not what you have to do," his mother said. "You can go to school and play music, too."

"No. This is it. I'm through. The only class I like is Mrs. Fly's. Other than that, school isn't for me. Playing music is what I was meant to do. Life is too short. I know that's a cliché, but I found that out today, Mama. Not only is tomorrow not promised, but the next sixty seconds is not even guaranteed. So I need to do what I can do while I can do it. I'm packing my guitar and hitting the road." Red ran his fingers through his red hair.

"Hitting the road?" She sounded as if her fingers were smashed beneath a rocking chair. "And just where are you going to live in Memphis, Brandon?"

"I don't know if I'll even live in Memphis, Mom. But Beale is my first stop. I know a couple of guys down there in the music and I'll hang with them until something better comes along.

"Until something better comes along?" She sounded as if she were massaging her bruised hand. "Brandon. Most people are trying to get away from living that way. You're trying to run to it. What kind of life is that?"

"I don't know. I haven't lived it yet. All I can say is that right now it's going to be my life."

Helen Whitby's tone became matter of fact. "Brandon Wilson Whitby, there has been a dentist in your family going all the way back to your great-grandfather. Have you thought about what this will do to your father? Do you think this would be fair to your family?"

Brandon contemplated eight more years of school,

driving to the office in the morning until he returned to the suburbs in the evening, the cocktail parties, civic clubs, church functions, cook-outs with colleagues, professional seminars, mindless vacations until he wanted to scream. He loved his father, but he had no desire to become him or do what he did.

"I don't think it'll be fair to my family if I did become a dentist. That's what everybody else wants and they can chase that dream if they want to, chase it all day long. But me, I'm going follow this music and see where it leads me."

"Blues music, Brandon? Besides B.B. King, who else makes a living playing that kind of music? Classical or rock, I could understand that. I wouldn't approve of it, but I could understand it. I guess I should be thankful you don't want to be a rapper or hip-hop mogul or something. And the places where that blues music is played is nothing more than a tinderbox waiting for a match to be struck. And if the place doesn't catch on fire, somebody is bound to get stabbed or shot or even worse. And Beale Street . . . that's a thug's paradise. If you want to be a mugger or want to be mugged, there's no better place than downtown Memphis. Beale Street is not safe for anyone anymore. Especially, someone like yourself."

Brandon laughed. "Sounds like you visited a spot or two back in the day, Mom. I don't think many of those places are still around. If there are, I sure wish I could find most of them. I'd love to play a juke in the early morning hours, smoke in the air and sawdust on the floor. But most of the juke joints now have been turned into trendy coffee shops or downtown cafés that cater to college kids like me on the weekends. Every now and then, you'll get lucky and find a festival somewhere in the middle of nowhere. But where I play is not a major concern for me. As long as I get to play is the only thing I care about. And for me, it's the blues or nothing. The blues is ground zero for the human condition. Every emotion you'll ever experience in your life is in that music. And when you finish listening to it, you'll feel a lot better. The only thing I found close to that is jazz. But the road to jazz has to come through the blues. I tell you, Mom, the blues were here before God got here."

"Brandon!" She screeched like a cat with bared fangs and arched back. "That's blasphemy!"

"Mom. After God created the world and everything in it in five days, He was lonely. Still lonely. What is that? That ain't nothing but the blues. So what did He do? Made Him a man and a wo-man to deal with them blues." He paused to amplify his words. "That's Bible."

"Brandon. I don't think that's sound Biblical doctrine. Matter of fact, I don't even think that's in the Bible at all. But that's understandable. You're in a very stressful situation right now and you're not thinking very clearly. It's a confusing time. There's no point in throwing your life away after some blues."

He sighed heavily. "You're right, Mom."

"Good," she sighed in relief.

"It's a lot I don't know, especially about the Bible. But I've never been more certain about hitting the road. This is what I have to do. The only way for me to find my life is to chase after some blues, as you put it. I'll either find it or it will find me. You worried about me going down to Beale and hanging out in Memphis. Well, Memphis is one stop, one stop where I can sign a record deal and then from there, who knows? But I will say this: I'm being held against my will in a classroom at a junior college in Stovall, Tennessee. Memphis ain't got nothing to do with that. Ain't nobody really safe, Mom. I don't care where you are."

"Oh, Brandon."

He knew that if his mother's voice had hands, it would grab him by the shoulders and try to shake sense into him.

"Don't you know you have people who love you? What about Kerri?"

What about Kerri? He had given much thought to her, to them and their future together. They had met two years ago in high school when he was a senior and she a sophomore. Now, she was in her senior year, number one in her class and had already accepted a scholarship to Duke. Every time he thought of her brown eyes and that dimple in her chin, he smiled. To ask her to change her plans and join him on the road would be as unfair to her as his parents wanting him to be a dentist and to try to have a long-distance relationship would be more unfair than that. She had a right to her own life, becoming a pediatrician just as her older brother had. Until now, saying goodbye to her was purely in his head and as long as he kept it there, it wasn't really real and as long as it wasn't really real, he was in total control of the situation. But now, the speaking of her name shattered all delusions and he couldn't dodge, duck or deflect reality anymore. It stood naked and shivering before him, stared him square in the mouth and dared him to speak. The break-up was unavoidable and inevitable. He thought about simply walking away without saying goodbye, but he knew there was not enough cruelty in his bones to do that. He could try to explain this, articulate that. Maybe she would understand, maybe not. But there was no easy way to do it. He would simply have to say, it's over.

"I don't know."

"This is going to break your father's heart, you know?"

"Where is my father? Let me speak to him."

"You have to be kidding me? Lionel Spann?" Robert Strother asked his wife a second time as if she were hard of hearing."

"No, I'm not kidding" Carol replied. I talked to Lionel Spann about two hours ago." She cleared her throat. "Why is that so hard to believe?"

"I was just thinking about him, probably about two hours ago. This guy, this kid with the gun reminds me a whole lot of him. That's incredible that he would call. I guess he's watching the news?"

"Yes, he's watching the news," she explained, "and remembered that you're in the Chamber program at Stovall State and wanted to make sure that you're all right. I told him that you were one of the people being held hostage at Stovall and that I pray you are all right, that he knows about as much as I do. When I told him that, the line went dead for a long time, like he had fainted or something. Anyway, when he came back on, he apologized for my trouble and wanted to know was there anything he could do for me."

Robert laughed softly. "Sounds like Spann. He's just a good guy." Robert found himself musing about former days.

"Well," she continued, "before he hung up he said that he wasn't at Telmark Foods anymore, that he was a manager at a warehouse that distributes books all over the world. He said that he's looking for a second shift supervisor and that the job is yours, if you want it."

"If I want it?" Robert repeated the question to convince himself that he had heard correctly. The room wavered through the tears in his eyes. His throat constricted and choked each sound before it became a word. When he was able to talk, the only words to escape his lips were "praise God." He felt like jumping up and down, running around the room shouting "hallelujah" and even giving Alex a big bear hug. Instead, he remained seated on the floor, closed his eyes and felt two warm streams roll down his cheeks. A job. Being a supervisor. A full-time job. After two years, a full-time job with benefits. He could be a man. Again. He, Carol and Amber could get a house of their own and in the backyard with a hammock beneath the shade of two trees, he could drink a cold beer while petting the Golden Retriever. At night, he and Carol would make love as if the world were coming to an end or the way they did when they were in their twenties and thought they'd never die. Later, Carol would lie in the crook of his arm as his woman; he would watch her drift into asleep, kiss her on the cheek as her man. In the morning, he would have his coffee black, pack a lunch, drive to that book distribution center as if he owned the deed to the City of Stovall. A job. A job would give him something to look forward to each morning and a sense of accomplishment at the end of the day. If nothing else, it would allow him to see respect once again in the eyes of his family when he sat across from them over supper.

"Robert?"

"Hey."

"Are you all right?"

"Yeah. I'm fine. I was just thinking . . . how are the girls?"

Carol hesitated.

"Carol? What about Amber and Chelsea?"

She collected courage for words. "Not well. When we found out you were a hostage, Amber went to pieces. We had to take her to the emergency room. Chelsea is driving up from Tuscaloosa and should be here in about an hour. Dad is here with me."

"Oh God," he breathed, clenched his teeth.

"Where's Amber now?"

"She's home with Mom now and doing better. She had to be sedated."

Robert felt unworthy of everything. Here he was fantasizing about himself and what he would do and how he would do it when all this was all over and the reality of the situation was that he may not even have anyone to do it with or to do it for. Suddenly, in a moment as lucid as a vision, he realized that besides God, his family was all he had. No matter how low he may have gotten emotional over the past two years, he could always lift his eyes and see the outstretched hands of his family waiting to lift him once again. They'd never turn their backs on him nor forsook him. Robert had faith in God and believed that in the future he would see God. But Carol, Amber, and Chelsea were the manifestation of God in his life, God's love he could touch and be touched by each and every day. The thought saddened, reminded him that he'd been given much, had taken much for granted.

"How are you doing, Carol?"

"I'm praying and holding on. I don't know anything else to do. Besides, Dad has been here with me from the beginning."

"Just exactly where are you?"

"We're outside looking up at your window. There's a crowd of people here. Cops and TV folks. I think a lot are family, but most appear to be just people waiting to see what happens. God. It's a mess out here."

"I can hear all the commotion, but everything's going to be all right, Carol. I'm going to get that job for me, for you and the girls. We'll find us a little quiet spot north of town and pretty soon you'll be able to quit work and stay home the way you used to do and we'll take that Alaskan cruise the way we talked about before all the glaciers melt and I saw a BMW for sale in this guy's yard just the other day---"

"Robert. Robert! We need to get you out of there safe and sound first."

He laughed easily as if he were reclined on a bed in a hotel room. "I told you everything is going to be all right. I love you. I love you so much that I'm going to walk out of here. All I need is for you to be waiting on me when I do. Will you be there, Carol?"

"The leaves are starting to change."

Megan Fly hesitated, groped at understanding through a dense fog. "What leaves, Michael?"

"All over the northeast. New Hampshire. Back home."

The word *home* spread warmly, settled sweetly in the bottom of her stomach. Soon, the holiday season would be upon us, Megan thought, and there would be weekends at the lake, pumpkins to carve, pies to bake, sleigh rides through the woods, decorations to hoist, a tree to trim, the embrace of family, the laughter of friends and resolutions to break. Other images materialized before her, but the mere thought of them brought melancholy to mind. These had become the things she cherished, the things she moved away from.

"What are you trying to say?"

"I'm saying that I want to go back home to paint the trees, the lakes, the countryside. I need to expand my portfolio with some landscapes. I can't think of a more beautiful place or time of year to do that than fall in New Hampshire." When she didn't answer, he asked again: "Can you?"

"No, I can't. But I think everything about the northeast is beautiful."

"I thought so. And I think to get back up that way for awhile would be a good thing too. When all this is over with."

"What about the farm, Michael?"

"I'm talking about when all this blows over. And it will. We're both gonna need a break and we can head back east for a week or two."

A week or two? Megan bristled at the idea. One or two weeks would only serve as a palliative for a home-sickness that required major surgery. "Michael. This is the beginning of the semester. I just can't take off for a week or two. I have an obligation to this school and more importantly an obligation to my students. And right now, Alex needs me more than any student I've ever had."

"Alex? Alex the hostage taker Alex?!"

"Megan," Michael spoke slow and deliberate. "Listen to me. Number one, that guy is not your student or anybody else's student . . ." He stopped in mid-sentence. "Has he tried anything?"

"No, Michael. He hasn't tried anything." The idea that her husband would harbor the idea produced disgust. "The only thing he has tried is to be a human being."

"A human being?! He sure as hell's not acting like one. Megan. You don't need to get too close to this guy. He's already tried to kill one woman and the next time he might get it right."

Megan studied Alex from across the room as if she were looking at him for the first time. "What are you talking about?"

"I'm talking about what's being reported on the news. I guess you don't know. But this guy's is a criminal, a dangerous criminal. And he's crazy to boot."

She looked away from Alex. "Yeah, well. I guess we all have a touch of that."

"Megan . . ."

"No, I don't know anything about him trying to kill anyone or the circumstances behind it or even if it's true. All I know is that this is still my classroom and I'm responsible for what goes on in it and the people who are in it. I'm the only thing between life and death for everyone in this classroom, including Alex."

"What about you?"

"What about me?"

"What's between life and death for you, Megan?"

She thought for a second. "Poetry." She measured her words more precisely. "It's not just what I do, it's what I am. As far as Alex goes, he may be dangerous, a criminal. He may even be crazy, but he's figured out one thing: he knows what he wants and he's not afraid to go after it."

"Megan. The last thing you need to do is start sympathizing with this guy."

"I don't know if I'd call it sympathy, Michael. But he, this situation, has made things a lot clearer and one of the things I'm certain about is that I don't need to go to New Hampshire right now or anytime soon."

"Why?"

"I may not come back."

Megan could almost hear his thoughts twisting and tangling in the silence. "What?"

"When all this is over, it's not a good idea for us to go anywhere. We need to be still. Talk."

"Is there someone else?"

"No," she laughed softly. "Just me."

"You sure?"

"If there was anyone else I wouldn't have tried to make your dreams my dreams. And for a while I did. But my own would never go away."

"I didn't know you were so unhappy."

"More restless, frustrated, even bored, than unhappy." She pondered the word *unhappy*. "I don't even know if I need to be happy to write. I just need to have joy when I do write." She changed the phone from one ear to the other. "You know I'm working on a new book of poems, don't you?"

"No. What's the name of it?"

"Dispatches from the Edge of Reason. I'm about three-fourths finished."

"Wow." He was more stunned than amazed. "I had no idea, Megan. Is there anything else I need to know?"

"That I love you and I love being married to you, but this place makes it hard to do either."

"All right," he said after a long pause, "you like the big city and I like the country life. We'll have to find some ground somewhere that both of us can share. Maybe a few months here, a few months there. You willing to do that?"

"That's one of the things we can talk about."

"In the meantime, what about the leaves?"

"I think you should paint 'em while they're still on the trees."

"I'm not going anywhere until I hold you in my arms. And when I do, that's going to be for a very long time."

Sara had hung up with her mother five minutes ago. She sat with bowed head as if praying or taking a nap, her clasped hands resting on her stomach. Each time the baby kicked, joy leaped within her. She wanted to tell Mrs. Fly, the class, run to the nearest window and fling it open, tell the whole world that there was life inside her. But most of all, she wished Nick were here and he, they, could place their hands on her stomach and feel the miracle together. The thought saddened her. The baby would kick again, but there would never be another first kick and he would never be a part of it. And what if he didn't make it home in time to hold her hand in the delivery room and welcome his son into the world? The thought of Nick not being there with open arms to catch their son after he'd taken his first steps made Sara want to cry. As quickly as she dismissed the notion, it returned back to her mind. She had to face that reality whether it was real or not: what if there was such a thing as life without Nick? She would become a widow before she even married. A widow raising a fatherless boy child. It had been done before. Her mom had raised her and her brother alone and the both of them had turned out all right, she'd thought. She and the baby would continue to stay with her mom until she walked out of Stovall State with a nursing degree. She chose nursing because there seemed to always be a shortage of nurses somewhere. She had to have that degree. The last thing she wanted to do was to work two or three nowhere jobs and still not have enough money to take care of the both of them. But enough of that kind of thinking. Nick was coming back, coming home and when he did, the three of them would be inseparable. He'd told her so. She closed her eyes and sealed his promise in her heart.

Sara rubbed her hands over her belly, whispered words to her child. She made vows of her own to provide for, love and protect his life. They had talked about a strong name like Joshua or Edward with its ring of royalty, but here in the chaos of a classroom, she had never been as clear as she had about anything in her life at this moment: It was the perfect name and the perfect choice. Why didn't she think of it before? The very thought made Sara smile and when she did, her son tapped her once again. "Don't worry about a thing, precious. I'll take care of you until your daddy comes home. I love you too."

"Alex. Alex?" Megan's voice traveled across a wide chasm, landed like an echo upon Alex's ear. He had been adrift in daydreams about his father. He wondered if he sported a beard these days or had a bald head like himself. Had he re-married? Did he, Alex, have a baby brother or sister somewhere in the world? Where did his father live? What kind of work had he done over his life? What were the things that gave him pleasure in that life? Was he still a fisherman? Did he ever think about the son he last saw at five years of age?

"Alex?"

When Alex followed the line of sound that carried his name, Megan held the other end. "Yes, Mrs. Fly."

"I believe you have more poems?"

"Yeah. Yeah, I do. But can I use your phone for a minute?" Alex gathered himself from the corner, grabbed the phone from her outstretched hand. Staring at the screen, he realized that the sheriff knew how to get in touch with him, but he didn't know how to contact the Sheriff. He knew Megan had just gotten off the phone and when he tapped the number below the first one, Sheriff Johnsey exploded in his ear before the phone even had a chance to ring.

"Alex! You must be a mind reader, son. I was just fixing to call you. How are you?"

"I need to talk to my Mama."

"Your mama wants to talk to you too. And you'll get the chance. But it needs to be face to face, son.

I can't send her in there. But you can come on out anytime you're ready. All I need is for you to let everyone come out first, hands up, and then you follow suit. You ready to do that?" Sheriff Johnsey looked over his shoulder at two TBI agents. The one in the blue suit, Burton, stood six feet tall with brown hair and broad shoulders. Burrows, his partner, wore a gray suit with a red tie, his face framed by a pair of square glasses. They scrutinized Sheriff Johnsey more than they observed him.

Alex breathed heavily. "I need to talk to my mama."

"Alex. I need you to let everybody go and come out and when you do you can say whatever you want to say to your mother for as long as you want to. I promise you that."

"I need to talk to my mama."

"When you going talk to me, son?"

"What I tell you about calling me, son?" He sighed again. "When I finish talking to her, I'll talk to you, Sheriff."

"Alex." The two syllables wrapped around his mother's voice sounded more like a plea than his name.

"How come he didn't want me, Mama?"

"Alex, baby. Who are you talking about?"

"My daddy. How come he didn't want me?"

"Oh, baby. We don't have time to deal with that right now."

"Why he walk out on me?"

"Alex, he walked out on you and me. But most of all he walked out on himself. It was him that needed you more than you needed him."

"Where he at now? He still living?"

"Yes. He's still living. Somewhere in Oregon, last I heard. I haven't thought about your daddy in a lot of years and I'm glad I haven't. Because when I do, I don't think about 'where he at now.' The question is where the hell has he been? Where was he when you had your tonsils taken out or where was he some Christmas morning or where was he on one of your birthdays. You made it through all of that ok. Matter of fact you owe your daddy a thanks. He taught you how not to be a daddy. So, just make sure when you have a son or a daughter that you're a part of their lives whether you live with them or not. You hear me?"

"How come that man didn't want me?"

"That man been gone over twenty years. You can't hold on to the wind, baby. Sooner or later, you got to let him go and live your own life. You're going to be ok. Everything is going to be ok. But first, you have to let those people go and come on out. Alex?"

Alex interrupted the long silence. "Tell the Sheriff I'll call him back in a minute." He snapped the gun out of his waistband, flipped off the safety. "Tobi? Tobi. Where you at?"

"I'm right here, van der Pool."

"Man, where you been? Why is it every fucking body want to run out on me?"

"Slow your roll, man. I don't know what you're talking about. I ain't been nowhere. Besides, you said you were Tobi, remember? How could I ever fucking leave you alone?"

"Tobi. You ever thought about killing yourself?"

"I'd be lying to you if I said I hadn't, van der Pool. And I think most folk would be bullshitting you too if they say they ain't. But I ain't never made no plans to do myself in, except that time some dope dealers had me trapped in an empty warehouse and I saved a bullet for that. But hell, I always wanted to live, man. One time I stole a car and had to bail when the cops starting chasing me. They fired at me and, I fired back at them trying to get away."

"Is there a crime you haven't committed, Tobi?"

There was a long silence while Tobi contemplated

an answer. *"Probably so, van der Pool. But when you come from a neighborhood with poor housing, poor schools, and little opportunities, sometimes committing a crime against society is the only way you have to fight back. If they going to kill you, at least you can get one good lick in before they nail the coffin shut. And I know what you're thinking, van der Pool: I ain't no natural born criminal. I was made into one. When you're Black in this country, you're always guilty of something until you prove you're not. All I ever wanted was to live, man. Live in a good neighborhood and have a good job and have plenty to eat and take care of my family. I didn't think that was asking a whole lot. Making chump change being a flunky for some of these white folks, I couldn't feel like a man living like that and if I had to live that way, I'd rather be dead. You might not believe this van der Pool, but I wouldn't mind going to college. I had to quit school when I was in the eighth grade because there wasn't enough money. Ain't never been enough. I just wanted to be free. But that's too much for some of these white folks to deal with. They think you want to take what they got. Some of them anyway."*

Alex closed his eyes, bent his arm at a forty-five degree angle with the gun in slow ascent towards his head.

"Alex."

"Van der Pool."

"Alex!"

"Van der Pool!"

"Van der Pool!"

"Alex!"

"Alex!"

"Van der Pool!"

Caught between the terror of the world being ripped from its foundation and the exhilaration of being a witness to it all, Alex stood in a vortex of brilliant flashes against the backdrop of his life. He was an eight-year-old child waiting to go fishing, a twenty-five-year-old man who had taken hostages and everything in between all at the same time. "What!" When he opened his eyes the room stopped spinning and there was only the voice of Megan to fill the void.

"The poetry."

Alex forced the gun back into his waistband, grabbed his book bag from a desk and extracted a handful of poems. He shuffled pages from one hand to the other and cleared his throat after choosing one. "Shackles of the Mind:"

I mirror before this stand
Called I see. My life and all
Is misery broken hearted
Staring misery back at me.
Of people my people – unwanted people,
Outcast people, oppressed people
Black people transplanted people,
In a white land, like freaks for pleasure
And display. Identity raped
With no 'nigger' that I know
Of. Dignity that was stripped of rape
By the master's crack of a master's whip,
Earth swallowed by the Blood
The sweat of the swallowed brow
From sunrise to sunset.
My shackles bound by ancestors
And life lived outside chains.
Sub-humans, disposable
To the consumption of time.
Now my fate I ponder in this
Land, for little has changed.
My well-defined is limited by that world
(see that line I only dream of crossing
I didn't think you would.)
But you can read the goddam sign!

When peace comes, Jesus will be done.
I will stand, until then find.
Bound and frustrated
These shackles of the mind."

"Thank you for sharing that, Alex." Megan looked at the students in the class and when no one responded, she called on Rose.

"Thank yall for letting me read it. But it you could, could you rip it apart. That's the only way I think I can get better. I don't want to be writing the same way this time next year."

"Well," Rose began, "the line 'transplanted in a white land like freaks' caught my attention. I think it's a good line and I think I understand what he's trying to say, but I think the poem would be stronger if there were more clarity there. For example, you would transplant flowers or shrubs and you would capture freaks if that's possible. So I think to solidify the point just eliminate 'transplant' and say 'captured into' maybe."

Alex slid a pen from his book bag and made notations on his paper.

"Word choice makes a difference. Poetry is about, among other things, an economy of words and each word, Alex. Each word has to be well spent and to the point. Don't use ten words when one word can say the same thing. That's a good observation, Rose" Megan added. "Brandon?"

"I loved the rhythm of people: unwanted people, outcast people, oppressed people, black people. If he could find a way to isolate that particular phrase, that might even strengthen the alienation that he's striving for in the poem."

Alex scribbled again.

"Excellent," Megan exclaimed. "Not only does

that part of the poem have rhythm and musicality, Brandon, but what else does repetition do for a poem? We've talked about this before with other poets we've studied."

"Well, when we're reading a poem like this with that kind of rhythm in it, its speeds you up, pushes you through the poem. Sort of like a chord progression on a musical scale. So by speeding up and slowing down later, you create tension in the writing."

"Very good. Alex?" Alex had his head bowed, trying to record each suggestion. "When you have time, investigate a technique call anaphora. That's where you repeat the same word or words, for that matter, at the beginning of two or three lines in a poem. It's another way of building rhythm in a poem as well."

He looked up briefly, continued to write in the margins of his page.

"Sara. Any thoughts?"

"Uh . . . I don't know." She pulled a strand of hair behind her left ear. "The end of the poem . . . I don't know if 'goddam' and 'Jesus' needs to be in the same line or even so close together. I haven't made up my mind if that works or not."

"That's ok," Megan smiled. "Let's look at it for a moment. When I heard Alex read it, it certainly caught my attention and I think everyone else's as well. And why is that? Glad you asked," she said with a wry smile. "Well, it's the sheer irony of the two words in close proximity of one another that creates a contradiction. He has something sacred in relation to something profane. In other words, we're back to tension again. The two words so close to each other push and pull against one another, which is always a good thing. Remember this Alex: that where you break a line is not as important as the line itself. Strive to make each line of your poem strong enough where it can stand on its own or be a poem all to itself. Understand?"

He nodded in her direction.

"Monte."

"I can dig the poem and feel what he's saying. I like the title a lot, a new kind of slavery. Cool. But like you always say Mrs. Fly," he turned his head in her direction, "the poem should tell us how the poet is feeling, the poet shouldn't have to tell us. He ends the poem with 'frustrated.' I got that. Everything that came before "frustrated' was frustrated, so he didn't need that in the end. I don't think."

"What Monte is alluding to, Alex, is imagery. Let the images in your poem be so stark and striking and compelling that words like 'frustrated' won't be neces- sary. Abstractions and value judgments only weaken the poem. Instead, employ rich and vivid metaphors and similes in your work to make the language power- ful enough to light a fire on the page. Or to put one out. But remember: the figures of speech have to be fresh and bold. And remember this as well: all poems are not easy to understand. Some poems you may not ever understand. But the way you know its poetry is by some of the things we have just spoken about. And of course, no clichés in poetry. OK?"

Alex took more notes.

"Mr. Strother. Your thoughts on 'Shackles of the Mind.'"

Mr. Strother cleared his throat. "Honestly?"

"Alex has come to us for help with his poetry," Me- gan replied. "The only way to do that is to be honest."

"Well," Robert began, "after the first four lines, I totally zoned out. Everything after that sounded more like propaganda than poetry. I felt like it became nar- row and exclusive. I appreciate the sentiment of the writing and I get just how bad a thing it used to be, but I didn't have anything to do with slavery. What am I as a white man supposed to do with that?"

"You didn't have to have anything to do with slavery," Alex stopped writing, looked Robert in the eye. "The way things are set up, being white comes with built-in perks and benefits today whether you like it or not. Talk about exclusive. You can thank slavery for that, Mr. Strother. You can get into some doors I can't even knock on."

Robert laughed. "Man, you got to be kidding me! Tell me where I can find a door like that? I haven't had a job in two years. I've lost just about everything and had to move in with my in-laws."

"Losing a job, losing everything and moving in with family, ain't nothing new to me. Right now, you're just in survival mode. But hell, man, that ain't nothing new either. I'm always trying to survive something the best way I can. Shit," he thought out loud, "it's a poem in there somewhere. Neither one of us might not be working, but we ain't never been unemployed the same way. Like I say, right now you're in survival mode, but you'll be ok. You got an insurance policy. Just stay white. It'll pay off sooner or later. You asked 'what are you supposed to do with that?' Whatever you want to. Slavery is part of my heritage, my culture, my pain. You or anybody else don't have to listen to it or read it. But if I want to write about it, I will. And if I want to write about it all day long, I will. Langston said in a manifesto once, something to the effect, that if white people or black people are pleased with what we write, that's ok. But if they are not pleased, then that's ok too. I don't ever hear anybody telling a Jewish person that they talk about the Holocaust too much. And if they would tell a Jewish person that, they'd be just as wrong as what you're saying to me."

"Alex," Robert had both hands out in front of him, "I'm not suggesting that you don't have the right to write what you want to write about. Everybody does. But the poem you just read reads like it was written during Langston's time. Things have had to have gotten better since then. I have a friend . . ."

"During Langston's time?" Alex's eyes flashed fire. "Man, the word *nigger* ain't never went out of style. Just depends on who's saying it and how they're saying it and most times the word don't even have to be said. It just is. You get rid of the word *nigger*, I don't think the country could stand it."

"I couldn't disagree more, Alex" Robert shook his head. "I think the country would be better off without it. I think we'd be better off without any kind of discrimination of any type." He hunched his shoulders, cast his eyes upon the floor. "I don't know. Discrimination comes in all shapes and forms. One of the reasons why I been out of work is because of my age. What am I supposed to do about that?" He looked up at Alex. "One thing I'm not going to do is become bitter. Got too many folks depending on me. I'm just one person. If I can treat the next person the way I want to be treated, that's all I can do. But maybe I'm just a dreamer."

Sara cleared her throat, spoke to no one in particular. "If treating someone the way you want to be treated is a dreamer, I wouldn't care to ever wake up. But that takes a lot of love to love yourself like that. And I will say this: I don't think anyone should tell you who you have the right to love or want to get married to."

"You got to be kidding me," Alex jumped in. "This is the South. We don't go for none of that gay stuff down here."

"Langston Hughes was gay," Monte blurted.

"Bullshit," Alex blurted back. He stared at Monte and the faces of other writers he admired materialized before his eyes: James Baldwin, Tennessee Williams, Audre Lorde. "Well," he blinked and they vanished back into nothing, "if he was and as good as he was, he had the right to be any goddam thing he wanted to be. By the way, I thought I told you to shut up." He put his hand on his gun.

Alex watched Monte's eyes settle on his gun. "Yo, dog," Monte ran his hand over his afro, "I been wanting to ask you something since you first pulled that unit." He nodded towards Alex's gun. "Why us? Why didn't you take a four-year college hostage? This a fucking junior college, man. It ain't really a real college. You want to be famous, that would've been the thing to do."

"What I do and where I do it ain't none of your goddam business. You're here at this junior college. Does that mean you ain't a real baseball player?" He didn't expect Monte to answer, didn't give him time to.

"OK, then, motherfucker. I'm a poet," Alex declared. "The last thing I'm worried about is being famous. I'll let somebody else deal with that. Ain't nothing wrong with a junior college. Hell, I don't know if I picked this place or this place picked me." His eyes scanned the five faces before him. "Mrs. Fly." He zoomed in on her. "What do you think about the poem?"

"Well, the first thing I want to say is that I'm really shocked and taken aback by what you said about gays. You mentioned discrimination and hatred against your own heritage and culture. So, how do you then discriminate or hate another group or culture?"

Alex looked at her, past her, towards the window and still could think of nothing to say. "I don't know." He threw up both hands. "I don't have anything against gays. Not outright, anyway. I'm still working all that out."

Megan smiled. "That's ok. Evolving is always a good thing. And I love the honesty, intensity, and passion you bring to your writing. But at some point, the work will benefit and will have more impact if you learn how to step back and put some space between yourself and what you're writing about. In other words, don't lose the fire that you have, but don't get burned by it either. Be objective in your subjectivity. Approach your work like an assassin—"

"Damn," Monte interrupted. "Don't say that, Mrs. Fly."

"Alright. A surgeon, then. A heart surgeon who every time he performs an operation saves a life. You believe that about poetry, don't you Alex?"

Alex looked up from taking notes. "Of course. If I didn't I wouldn't be here."

"Good." Megan crossed her legs lotus-style. "Another thing you need to consider is form. Can I see how you have the poem structured on the page, please?" She stretched her hand towards him and when the paper was in her grasp, said thank you. She perused his work and gave it back to him. "All right. Two things: The first would be the actual lines in the poem themselves. Don't focus so much, Alex, on where or how you break a line. But focus on the line itself. After all, the basic element of a poem is the line. Juxtapose words to create contrast and let that line and all your lines be a poem all by themselves. The other thing would be the form of the poem. Because of the subject matter, I think the poem would be best served with quatrains or four-line stanzas. Let the white space on the page be just as important as what you have written on the page. The white space is silence or a natural pause; use it to your advantage. In other words, the way the poem is laid out on the page should compliment what's on the page. The ways we say something is often times what we say. Somewhere along the line, you may hear that form is content. And that could be true. For example, if you write a sonnet, your content and what you have to say is restricted by fourteen lines in rhymed iambic pentameter. So, my advice would be, don't restrict yourself by laying the words on the page the same way all the time. Looking at the form of this poem, keep in mind contemporary poets very rarely capitalize the first word of each line. So as it relates to form, each poem lives and breathes on its own. Let it have its own life. That make sense?" She saw the wrinkles in his forehead. She'd just given him a crash course in a graduate school creative writing program and realized that what he needed most was a starter kit.

Alex liked the idea of using the 'white space' as she called it, to be invisible words. Cool. Other than that, the other things she said sounded like a foreign language with a few recognizable words here, a discernible phrase there. "Kinda sorta." He scratched out a few more notes, walked over to the desk and laid pen and paper upon it. He looked up and out as if it was the last thing he'd ever do. "All right. I got a couple more, but it's getting late. I told the sheriff I'd call him." Alex picked up the phone when it rang in his hand.

"Hey, Sheriff. You remember me?"

"Alex? What's this about?"

"I remember when I was in the seventh grade me and some of my friends skipped school one day and you saw us and tried to take us to a juvenile. Man, we must've known some streets you didn't know 'cause you never did catch us that day. You remember that?"

"You got me on that one, Alex."

"How you doing, Sheriff?" Alex paced the room

from door to windows, peeked between the blinds.

"Tired. And getting older by the minute. You've interrupted a whole day of fishing for me. A good day of fishing. I didn't think you were going to call me back." A few feet away, Burton and Burrows had their hands in their pockets, the heads bowed and their conversations lowered.

Alex stopped in the middle of the room as if the floor were flypaper. "Fishing? What kind of fishing?"

The sheriff laughed. "Hell, ain't but one kind of fishing, son. You bait the hook and throw it in the water. I usually hang out somewhere around the Forked Deer River. You should know where that is?"

"I do. What kind of fish they got in that river?"

The sheriff paused for a second. "Mostly cat and brim. Every now and then you'll pull a few Buffalo out of there." He paused longer this time. "You a fisherman, Alex?"

"When do you go? Morning or afternoons?"

"The earlier the better for me. I used to get up around 5 and head out. Nothing like watching the sun come up on a cool, crisp fall morning. Like watching God flip the switch on the world. You're sitting there and the trees light up, animals are reborn and being in the middle of all that makes you realize that you're alive. Really alive. Always have preferred country living to city life. But like everybody else, I'm getting old, Alex. No more five in the morning for me. After breakfast, I strike out about eight, nine now. Don't guess it really matters. Fish are a lot like us. If they're hungry, they're going to eat no matter what time of day it is, huh?"

Alex swallowed. "Early in the morning sounds like a good time to do anything. You always go by yourself?"

"Yeah . . . well . . . me and my boy David used to meet up there quite regularly, but now it's mostly by myself."

"Your boy move out of town?"

Alex listened as the background noise drowned out the silence. When Sheriff Johnsey spoke his words were gray and heavy. He laughed in spite of himself. "Yeah. Moved out of town. That's one way to put it. I lost David in a car wreck a year ago last month." He paused as if saying it made things permanent. "He was on his way home from a business meeting in Oxford and for some reason decided to take Highway 18 instead of the interstate. But he always did like the back roads, the scenic route he called it. That particular day, a deer dashed across the road and a lady coming in the opposite direction tried to dodge it and ran head on into my boy. The lady survived, my boy died at the scene.

"For about three months, I drove out there and parked on the side of the road where the accident happened and would just sit. I would sit there and talk to David until finally, I heard him say just as clear as you're talking to me Alex, he said Daddy, either you need to be locking up bad guys or fishing. Ain't no point to coming out here every day. Who you talking to anyway? Can't be me 'cause I ain't out here." Sheriff Johnsey's laughter sounded to Alex like water flowing over rocks in a shallow stream. "So, I listened, Alex. For a long time, I promised that I wouldn't go near a lake or river again, even locked my gear up in storage and gave serious consideration to selling it or giving it all away. But David was right and I listened. He would never be found on some two-lane State highway. When I finally got up enough courage to load up my gear and head out in the pickup toward the riverbank, he was right there waiting on me. He'd been there all the time, had never gone anywhere since he was about seven or eight years old and we first went out there all those years ago. So, I make it a point to head to the river at least once a week, more if I can fit it in. Some days I've pulled some big cats outta that muddy river, Alex; half of 'em I toss back 'cause the wife don't want to fool with 'em. Other days, I'm lucky to snag a hubcap or leather boot. But every time I'm on that riverbank, I hear David's voice in all the memories we shared out there. He was practically raised on the riverbank and I got a deeper sense of being a father being at his side. You got kids, Alex?"

"No. No kids."

"Yeah, well. You're young still. You got plenty of time for all that. And when you do, you'll find out it's one of the best things that could happen to a man."

"I don't know, sheriff," Alex mumbled. "Depends on who the man is."

"You got a good point there, son. I think you have a lot of good points and to be honest with you, this is really the first time I've talked about David openly like this. I guess it'll be the thing I'll wrestle with until I leave this earth. For me to have to bury my son, my only son, just goes against the natural order of how things should go. Hell, it was supposed to be the other way around. I lost a son and gained a daughter-in-law out there on that highway. They were planning on having kids, so everybody's struggling. But Rachel is talking about moving back home to be close to her folks and who can blame her for that. That's good for her. But me? I ain't got no place to go but to stay here with the wife. You heard the expression, 'play the hand you've been dealt?' I know what it is like to stare at a bunch of crummy cards, Alex. But I can't fold. Ain't no telling when I'll be holding a royal flush. Guess we're in the same boat, huh, son? We've both opened big shiny boxes only to find them empty. But you're in a way better position than I am. You got a lot of future in your future. Me? This is the

179

end of the road for old Sheriff Johnsey. I'm retiring. You're the first one to know that too. It'll just be me and David by the riverside. Every day."

Sheriff Johnsey coughed, spat on the ground. "All right, son. That's my story. Now tell me: what do you want?"

"I want to talk to my mama."

"No. You've already done that. So, what do you want?"

"I want to write poetry."

"You've had your poetry and you will have poetry. What do you really want, Alex?"

"I want to go fishing."

Sheriff Johnsey grimaced, looked up at the window to room 223. "I haven't lied to you and I'm not going to start now. I don't know how that'll all play out if it'll play out at all, but yes Alex, if the time and circumstance lends itself, you can have your fishing. I'll take you myself. We'll go out early in the morning and stay out there all damn day. Right now, no one has gotten hurt. So it's not as bad as you think. But the outcome depends on you. Everything depends on you." When Sheriff Johnsey looked for the two TBI agents, they were gone.

Alex walked over to the window and looked through its blinds. He searched for Sheriff Johnsey. He wondered what the Sheriff really looked like if his rough gravelly voice matched the facial features Alex had given him. What did his eyes look like? Could they bore through steel doors or make you smile in spite of yourself? And would the Sheriff smell like tobacco or liquor or cheap cologne as they rode together in the pick-up truck towards the fishing hole? Laughter over the phone was one thing, but did his whole body shake when he did so? Alex looked left, right, found the outline of a man in the distance talking on a cell phone.

"Sheriff. I'm coming out."

"All right," Sheriff Johnsey said it as if the word was a benediction to a prayer. "This is what I need you to do. . ."

". . . All right. I'll do what you want me to do. Give me a minute to say goodbye to everybody. I'll call you back and then we'll come out one at a time."

"Say goodbye?"

"It's a couple people I want to thank."

Sheriff Johnsey hesitated until an old saying that had been around for as long as he could remember blossomed in his head: all over but the shoutin'. It was over. He'd won. No one had gotten hurt, including himself. What the hell? He had waited it out this long. What were another few minutes? "Alex."

"Yeah, Sheriff?"

Sheriff Johnsey wanted to tell Alex that he was sorry that he'd hit him with the nightstick, sorry for all the Alexes he'd hit over the years with that same night-stick and as bad as he wanted to ask for forgiveness, he couldn't make himself say the words. "All right, Alex. But don't keep me waiting like the last time, now."

"Tell my Mama I love her." Alex hung up the phone as the sheriff was in mid-reply, continued looking out the window.

As soon as Sheriff Johnsey finished his conversation with Alex, he was summoned to a trailer that served as the TBI command center. On the way, he saw Eddie Reed, Johnnie Gardner, Tim Swinford and Marvin Bradbury huddled in a semi-circle their hands in their pockets. He nodded in their direction and they grimaced back at him. When Sheriff Johnsey walked in the door, Burton stood with his back to him, his face concentrating on a laptop. Burrows reviewed floor plans with three men holding rifles. Several others wore headphones and were talking into microphones. "Sheriff," Burton said, "we're taking over the situation."

"We? Taking over?" Sheriff Johnsey's mouth hung open long after his words were gone.

"Yes. The TBI is officially in charge."

"Look, that's not necessary, Special Agent," Sheriff Johnsey pleaded. "Van der Pool has agreed to surrender. I got him."

Agent Burton snapped the laptop shut, spun around and faced the Sheriff. "He's been surrendering all day, man. We don't know if you got him or he has you. But we're not waiting any longer to find out. You're off the case."

"Off the case my ass. I've been negotiating all day with this kid and no one has gotten hurt. Now we're down on the one-yard line and you sonsofbitches want to take it in for the score. You're full of shit, Burton."

Everyone in the room looked in their direction.

Burrows walked over to where the two men were standing. When he got within feet of them, Sheriff Johnsey sized him up, quipped: "You look even more impacted than him."

"That's enough, Sheriff," Agent Burton shot back. "I shouldn't have to remind you that the State in Stovall State is just that. This is State property and beyond your jurisdiction. We thought that you could handle it, but we thought wrong. This has gone on longer than it should have and it damn sure isn't going past this night."

"I agree," Sheriff Johnsey said. "It's not going past this night. It's not even going past the next hour. I got him. You heard what he said. He said he's coming out. You rush him now, nobody in that room will make it out alive."

"We've heard exactly what he's said and every time he says it he calls back to say it again. And now if he ever comes out, he wants to go fishing." Agent Burton said it loud enough for his colleagues to hear and they snickered.

Sheriff Johnsey cut his eyes from Burrows to Burton. "You think old Johnsey's a joke, huh?" He pointed his finger at Burton's nose. "Don't fuck with me, Burton. You know good and well that this kid's not well. He's hearing voices and talking back to 'em. That boy needs help. He don't need to be locked up or hurt no more."

Burton smiled. "All right, Sheriff. I apologize. I didn't know you cared about Black people so much. I guess after this you'll probably join the NAACP and start singing Kumbaya or something." Everyone laughed, stopped as quickly as they started. "We know he's hearing voices," Burton continued, "and at this point, Sheriff, we think that your voice hasn't added much clarity to the situation. You've built up a rapport with him and hell, that's good. You can adopt him when all this is over for all we care. But you've made us look like a bunch of red-neck, country hicks in front of the whole world and the TBI can't afford to be made to look like a bunch of red-neck, country hicks. Now," Agent Burton turned his back on the Sheriff and began to walk away, "if there's nothing else, there's a guy, crazy or not crazy, who's holding a classroom hostage that I must deal with."

Sheriff Johnsey cleared his throat. "Yeah, there's one more thing, Burton."

Agent Burton walked back towards the Sheriff. "What is it?"

Sheriff Johnsey drew back his right arm and when he brought it forward landed his fist on the side of Agent Burton's face. The room burst into a tumult of curses, shouts, things overturned. Two agents held Sheriff Johnsey by both arms

"Get that sonofabitch out of here!" Agent Burton commanded, rubbing his right jaw.

Alex opened the blinds halfway to get a better look at the four figures he thought were his mother, sister, step-father and one that moved like Delilah. But their forms were clouded in shadow and they could've been anybody. The only thing he could make out was the logo of Channel 6 in neon letters on the side of the night. In front of the news truck, Alex saw a Hispanic female reporter who had a microphone shoved into the face of a black man in a three-piece suit. He used his hands to punctuate his words.

"This proves my point," he said, pointing up towards the classroom window.

"So, Doctor Harnett, you're telling us that racism-related stress is the cause of the hostage situation we've had here for the past eight hours?" The reporter wore a dark green blazer and her brown hair neatly trimmed on her shoulders.

"Yes. That's one point of contention. We live in a society that reminds you that if you're different or anything other than white, just how different you are. The reminders may not be of a conscious nature—sometimes they are—but more often than not they're of the subconscious variety."

"For example?"

Dr. Harnett cleared his throat. "For example, the standards of beauty in this society have always been blonde hair, blues eyes and thin lips. This is something that no one has to tell you if you're a person of color, you learn it through osmosis from magazine photos, television, movies, etc. Also, consider that if you're a member of a race, and I used that word loosely, and that race has been historically and contemporarily portrayed as lazy, violent, criminal, incompetent or sexually promiscuous, then this becomes a stress factor as well. The dominant white society will never experience, or for that matter, never fully understand this."

"But what we do understand, Dr. Harnett," she pulled the microphone away from him, "is that there is such a thing as personal choice and our alleged perpetrator, who has a prior record, has chosen to hold hostage, at gunpoint, at least five other human beings. How do you explain other young black men who have not made similar choices?"

The doctor laughed to himself. "Whether they've made similar choices or not, gone to Harvard or a correctional facility, the stress factors from racism remain the same and, if there is no support from the community, a religious organization, or family structure, then it becomes just that much more easy for one to fall prey to depression, rage, hopelessness, paranoia. These symptoms have a tendency to manifest themselves in homicide, suicide, and substance abuse. I don't think it's a coincidence that African Americans suffer at higher rates from high blood pressure and cardiac diseases—more so than other ethnic groups."

"But doctor, we're a country of ethnic groups. The Irish, Italians, Polish, Jewish, the Germans have all come to this country and suffered some type of physical and psychological difficulties, but they rose above it. Are you saying that African Americans are not capable of rising above the past?"

"No. What I am saying is that the past has to be

dealt with openly and honestly before African Americans can begin to heal themselves. No one else can do it because unlike those other ethnic groups you named, only African Americans have withstood 245 years of slavery and another 100 years of de facto slavery followed by years of repressive Jim Crow and Black Codes legislation."

"Slavery, Doctor Harnett?!!

"Yes. Slavery. First of all, we must understand that slavery was built upon the financial exploitation of African Americans and the fallacy of white supremacy. So, black people's first experience in this country means that they were regarded as less than human beings and as far as the black man goes they were emasculated both physically and psychologically to neutralize them as a threat. This experience although centuries ago, is not that far removed from the African American psyche today and may never be. You mentioned other ethnic groups, Ms. Sanchez, who've had to overcome trials and difficulties and rightfully so. But those groups had a culture and a history to ground them in America while they were being mistreated. African Americans had no such luxury to fall back on. Their culture, history, and religion were destroyed in order to make them slaves and everything they created for and about themselves came right from the American soil itself. Now couple this with years of poor living conditions, chronic unemployment, inadequate schooling and violence from without the community, I submit to you that the majority of African Americans are suffering from PTSD."

"Post Traumatic Stress Disorder?"

"Or Post Traumatic Slavery Disorder."

"I want to come back to that, but you mentioned violence from without the community. Is it not true that black-on-black crime is more of a threat to the physical well-being of African Americans than violence from whites?"

"No. You are absolutely incorrect. Truth of the matter is that if I'm black and live in a black neighborhood, odds are if I am the victim of a crime, it'll be by another black person. Same scenario applies if I'm a white person living in a predominantly white neighborhood. The perpetrator in all probably will be white. So, this whole idea of black on black crime is basically a distraction from the real issue."

She coughed uncomfortably, removed an errant strand of hair from her eyes. "Doctor, you alluded to PTSD. That sounds like to me, and I'm sure a lot of our viewers would agree, an excuse to do nothing. Or to give up even."

"I think not. African Americans have had ample opportunities to give up and haven't done so yet. In fact, considering our history in this country, it's a miracle we're still around at all."

"But, Doctor, when you make a statement like that, you negate the fact that there is an Oprah Winfrey, a Condoleezza Rice or a Doctor Ben Carson and the tremendous accomplishments they have achieved. I think even you belong in that category."

Doctor Harnett shook his head. "No, the last thing I would want to do is to disparage the accomplishments of the people you've mentioned. But I don't think they'd want to consider themselves representative of an entire people either. They're brilliant individuals. And that's the thing. These individuals are often held up as exceptions. But whatever they accomplish doesn't negate the fact that the majority of African American are suffering and continue to suffer from the deleterious effects of racism in this country. And even the people you mention with all their success and wealth are not immune to not being allowed access to certain stores or being pulled over by police without provocation. Personally, I'm a trained psychologist with my own practice, and I've experienced my share of walking into places where I've not been wanted. And the police have harrassed me as well. But the worst thing I think I've ever dealt with is after giving a speech at a particular function is to have a white person come up to me and tell me how articulate I am. That happened so frequently that I no longer accept such invitations."

"Finally, you mentioned the 'real issue'." What is the real issue and what is the real solution?"

"The real issue is white supremacy. Racism just happens to be a by-product of that. This harkens back to the founding of the country when the idea of white superiority became entrenched within every American institution, even the Constitution. Remember, a great number of the founding fathers were slave owners. Yes, I know what your next question is, and the answer is yes. Things have gotten better. But at the same time, they've gotten worse. The criminal justice system immediately comes to mind. But what you and the viewing audience should understand. . ." he looked directly into the camera, ". . .is that white supremacy not only psychologically damages the minds of black Americans but it does an equal amount of damage, if not more so, to white Americans as well. This whole idea of white supremacy deflates the value of lives for people of color and inflates it for those of white people."

"All right, Dr. Harnett. You've told us, in your opinion, what the problem is. What is the solution?"

At four p.m., Delilah Jones returned from Nashville and remained motionless in front of the TV as if it were a watch, swinging back and forth. She sat hypnotized by its live and breaking news. A co-worker had phoned while she was on the road, exclaimed that Stovall was the capital of the country, would be on the map forever today. She'd dropped her bags, including the one with a gift for Alex, beside the front door when she entered her home and immediately dove for the remote control. She told herself over and over that it couldn't be the guy, the same guy she'd met earlier today. It couldn't be the same guy she'd given a ride across town. That guy had a vulnerability that made him all the more attractive to her. That guy loved poetry, the arts, possessed a sensitivity that she rarely found in any man she met today. That guy had promised to phone later, whose voice could charm her way past her bedtime. That guy that she thought she could hold hands and take long walks with. Days at museums, nights at the theatre spent with that guy. That guy. That guy would nibble her fingers as she fed him grapes from a picnic basket down by the lake at the park. That guy would sit beside her in the convertible with the top down on a clear night at the end of town and help her name the stars. That guy determined to work his way through college to become that guy. It just couldn't be Margaret's brother from down the road. As she continued to stare at the screen, she couldn't help but think of that same guy etched into the side of time standing in the morning sun waiting her to descend front porch steps as if she were the only person in the world he'd been waiting for all his life. That guy with the beautiful bald head.

Delilah listened to Dr. Harnett, whose eloquence and cadence reminded her of a Baptist preacher. He brought to mind a scripture she'd often heard while sitting in the pews: "Faith without works is dead." She had to do something. If only she could talk to Alex or simply write him a letter or maybe if he just saw her face. She had to go out to that college. Not to do so felt like a sin.

Dr. Harnett paused, began to expound upon the solution. Delilah grabbed the remote from the coffee table when a black man with dreadlocks dashed across the screen and snatched the microphone from the reporter. Over her screams, he shouted into the camera: "I'm that nigga I'm that nigga I'm that nigga!" before being wrestled to the ground by police. She pushed the off button and rushed from the house before the screen went black.

26

"Tobi."

"Alexander van der Pool."

"Thank you." Alex moved away from the window, backed himself into a corner.

"What's that all about?"

"You saved my life."

"No, man. You saved your own life. I told you once, I'll tell you one more time. I'm just a voice in your head and if I'm in your head, that means that I really don't exist unless you allow me to then it's your own voice you are listening to anyway. Look at you. You wanted to be seen, wanted to be heard like everybody else. A motherfucker's got to be deaf and blind not to know who you are now. You owe me nothing, man. Matter of fact, I'm in your debt. Lot of folks gonna know who I am a long time after this from now on. Like me or not, I ain't going nowhere."

"Yeah. I've been thinking about that too, Tobi. What if I was wrong? What if I'm just another selfish bastard? What gives me the right to come in here and do something like this? These people ain't done nothing to me. Poetry is a lot of things and one of the things it is is a mirror. I got a lot of work to do on me, Tobi. I don't know where I'm going and how I'll end up there. Sometimes I feel like there ain't no such place as there."

"That's being black in America, van der Pool. You're a citizen, but you're always being asked for I.D... You got freedom of speech, but they'll cut your tongue out one way or the

other and then name a street after you. The American dream has always dangled from the end of a stick and every time you reach for it, something moves it out of the way. I heard all that talk about life, liberty and the pursuit of happiness. And it's yours, as long as you chase after it in the ghetto. It's the home of the free, land of the slave. The state penitentiary is the new master now. Strange place, this America, van der Pool. It's the only place I know where you can be the President one day and be hunted down in the streets on that same day. It's the same old lynch mob, man. Except they don't need trees no more."

"I don't know, Tobi. Some days are so heavy and dark, I have to talk myself into breathing. Other days, feels like I don't belong no place at all. Like I'm in the way of myself or something. If not that, feels like I'm a leaf being blown every which way at the same time by the edge of the wind."

"Hey, man. You're in a long line of people who have felt like that and when you look over your shoulder, you'll see a whole lot more behind you. But through that and everything else, van der Pool, we be. That's all this world has given us. We be. As far as feeling like a leaf being blown by the edge of the wind, van der Pool, after this shit you done pulled off today, you are the edge of the wind."

"I'm going to call it a day, Tobi. I got what I came for."

"All right, man. It's your day to call. We'll meet up somewhere. You know where to find me."

Alex rolled his eyes toward the ceiling, closed them. When he opened them, he stared into five faces eager with anticipation. "If I give you something, will you give it to the right person when all this is over?" He called to Megan from across the room.

Megan realized he addressed her, stammered a response before answering. "Yes. Of course, Alex. Who am I to give what to?"

"Give me a few minutes," he said. Alex grabbed his book bag from the desk, retrieved pen and paper from it. He set the gun on the corner of the desk and tossed the bag atop an adjacent desk. He lowered his head and wrote across the page:

Is there anything lovelier than you?
Your beauty intimidates, until I know
Not what to do

How divine to plant a kiss upon your face
Exchange I love you's, wrap my arms
Around your waist

I long so much to hold your hand
With your every word
Being my command

For you are a queen
So graceful, so fine
Forever and always on my mind

Your smile, when directed my way
Makes the sun shine
Through eternity and a day

This pen may cease to give ink
But you, my love, will continue
To be of every thought I think.

When finished, Alex leaned back and held the paper at arm's length, silently read his words to himself. "Do you have an envelope?"

Megan nodded towards her desk. "Should be one in the letter holder."

Alex folded the poem in three parts, slid it inside the envelope before sealing it with saliva. He flipped it over, wrote Ms. Delilah Jones on the other side, walked over to Megan and put it in her hand.

"Where do I find this person, Alex?"

Alex stood over all six hostages, panned left and rested his eyes upon Sara. "You know, I haven't been quite able to figure you out. Sometimes when I look at you, you look pregnant; other times you don't. Are you?"

Sara smiled, said softly, "yes."

All faces in the room turned with raised eyebrows and congratulated her.

"You want a boy or a girl?" Alex asked.

"It's a boy. His name is Nick, junior."

Alex looked at Monte. "You know dog, you'd be a good man if I could shoot you once a day. " When he saw that Monte didn't know if he were joking or not, he tried to put him at ease. "I came close today, but I would've regretted it. Would have never gotten the chance to see you in the Big Leagues. Who you want to play for?"

"I like the Red Birds, but I'll make all of them better."

"No doubt." Alex scrutinized Robert's attire, tried to size him up by his designer buttoned-down shirt. "What kind of work did you do?"

"Ever heard of Telmark Foods?"

"The factory?"

"Yep. One and the same."

Alex had guessed wrong. He saw Robert behind the desk at a bank or investment company maybe. "Factory work is about like driving a truck. One day, you're behind the wheel and the next day you're hitch-hiking on the side of the road. But if you keep moving in the right direction, something bound to come along."

"The same goes for you too, Alex," Robert replied.

Alex nodded in his direction, looked at his reflection in the top of Rose's bald head. "You finished with your treatments?"

"The radiation, yes. But two more rounds of chemo are left."

"After that, what?"

Rose paused. "Tomorrow. Just tomorrow, Alex. There's always a tomorrow somewhere."

"Red. Man, you got some mean chops, son. Where you cop them skills?"

"I got a long ways to go, man. My mama started me playing the piano when I was eight. I hated it then, but I need to thank her now."

"I think your journey ain't as long as you think. Will you sign your CD for me when it comes out?"

"You got it, man."

Alex stood over Megan, extended his hand to her. "You don't have to worry about finding that person, Mrs. Fly. She'll find you." She placed her hand in his and he gently squeezed it. "Can I borrow your phone one more time, please?"

He moved back towards the window, looked outside while making a phone call. "Sheriff. Sheriff Johnsey? This Alex. I'm ready."

"Hello, Alex." The voice sounded cold and rigid as if it were detached from a human being and had a life all of its own.

Alex felt the air being sucked from the room, the night sag. Something edged up the back of his neck. "Who this?"

"Alex. This is Henry Burton with the Tennessee Bureau of Investigation. I'm the new negotiator."

"Negotiator? What was wrong with the old negotiator? Put the Sheriff on the phone."

"No. I can't do that, Alex."

"Where's Sheriff Johnsey?"

The voice on the other end cleared its throat and when it did it sounded like a machine changing gears. "The Sheriff's no longer here, Alex. He's called it a night. He's gone fishing."

Alex wanted to scream at the voice that that was a lie, that everything was a lie, that the Sheriff wouldn't abandon him, that he would be the first one to greet him when he walked out with his hands in the air, that the Sheriff preferred to fish in the fresh hours of the morning and promised to take him with him. Instead, when he turned around, Sara had her hand on the doorknob and was halfway out of the door. Alex yelled at her, rushed to pick up the desk and by the time he hurled it at the door, she was gone. "That's right, Sara," he shouted. "Go ahead and run out on me like everybody else. I'm used to it. I don't need you."

Alex picked the gun up from the floor, pointed it at the hostages and backed his way up against the windows. "I don't need nobody." He aimed the weapon at the door and waited. It could have been a second or an eternity, but everything froze in time until he heard the rumbling of feet outside the door and the world began to fast forward. "All right. I ain't dead yet, you motherfuckers." He gripped the pistol with both hands, thought about McKay's sonnet. "If we must die, let it not be like hogs/hunted and penned in an inglorious spot/while round us bark the mad and hungry dogs/making their mock at our accursed lot." He looked wildly around the room. "Tobi? You got to carry it, Tobi!"

"Van der Pool. Get away from that window!"

Alex didn't know if the incessant pounding was in his head or coming from somewhere else until he saw the door splintering, heard its hinges cringe. "Red. I need you to blow, man. Play me some of them blues you got in your pocket. Red!"

Red cupped the harmonica to his lips and began a ditty in 4/4 time.

"Tobi. You got to carry it." Alex's laughter drowned out everything but the music. "Yeah. I like that one, Red. *Sitting on Top of the World.* Ain't that Sonny Terry and Brownie McGhee?"

"Van der Pool. The desk. Get behind a desk, van der Pool."

Alex pulled the trigger and the gun responded with a hollow thud. Misfire. He tossed it aside and held his hands in the air. He threw back his head and laughed until the ceiling blew away, windows shattered, walls collapsed and smoke filled the room. A bolt of lightning struck him in the chest and as he was falling to the floor more fire tore through his abdomen and left a hole in his back. The shrill cries of his hostages and the curses of men rushed the room. Red clutched his left leg, rolled across the floor, hollered "I'm hit I'm hit!" and moaned himself into a corner. Megan massaged the pain in her right shoulder, figured the stress of the day had finally caught up with her. But when she removed her hand and saw blood on her fingers, she screamed.

"Van der Pool!"

Alex made out Tobi's outline hovering over him. He wanted to grab him by the lapel, but only had the strength to whisper. "Tobi. You got to carry my body. That's the only way to be free."

Alex's head moved slightly to the left, stared at Tobi as if his eyes were propped open. *"It's ok, van der Pool. You were free. If it wasn't for just a few hours. That's more than most people know in their whole lives."*

Tobi took his thumb and index finger and placed them like pennies upon Alex's eyes.

Three days later, Sheriff Warren Johnsey tossed his fishing gear into the back of his pickup and left the house at six o'clock in the morning. He'd showered and dressed in the pre-dawn, ignored his wife's heavy-eyed inquiries about where he was going with that beer under his arm before closing the door behind him. Neither did he bother to stop by the Downtowner for breakfast and bullshit. He hadn't heard from the fellows since the standoff and didn't know when he'd see them again. When Sheriff Johnsey passed the Stovall Examiner, the headlines from the past few days emblazoned across his windshield.

He didn't need a newspaper to read between the lies. He became infuriated all over again at the TBI's initial report that Alex grew increasingly erratic, had started shooting hostages and that's why a sniper collected him in the crosshairs of his rifle while the SWAT team rushed the room shooting what they could barely see. No one had to tell him that the only bullet Alex fired, forensics found lodged in the ceiling, and that it was police issued weaponry that shot Brandon Whitby and Megan Fly. Whitby got the worst of the two from a bullet that ricocheted off the floor and exited his thigh. He was still hospitalized. According to the paper, he had written a ballad about Alex and would tell the whole story of what really happened once he got his hands on that "harp" again. Mrs. Fly suffered a flesh wound to her shoulder and was released the same day. Since school was closed for the week, she and her husband pulled the Harleys out of the barn and had gone riding. In fact, Sheriff Johnsey learned more from the daily paper about the hostages than he really cared to know: Rose Verdell would be skydiving next week. Robert Strother was a Golden Gloves champion. Sara Carter was afraid of needles and Monte Merriweather was on the debate team in high school.

He could feel the agony in Edna Madison's plea of why was it necessary to kill her boy and for the State to turn over the body so she could provide a proper burial. There was warmth in Margaret's reminiscence of the time Alex was a teenager and had come upon a pit bull struck by a car on the side of the road. He labored a half mile with the wounded animal in his arms to the veterinarian's office and later paid the bill with his allowance money. Salvador wished that he had told Alex that he was going to start his own window cleaning service and asked him to be a partner sooner and maybe things would have been different. All three family members threatened to talk to the Stovall Examiner until it ran out of ink and if it did, they promised to find an attorney with a ball point pen.

The day before yesterday, Delilah Jones walked up the road and stopped at Margaret's house. In her hand was a copy of Pablo Neruda's *Twenty Love Poems* that she'd found in a used bookstore in Nashville. "This is for Alex," she said after Margaret invited her in and they hugged. Margaret accepted the book and when she returned from the bedroom there was a white envelope in her hand. "Megan Fly has been looking for you. She found me instead." She handed the envelope to Delilah. "This is for you," Delilah told the press it was none of their business what Alex had written, only that when she read the letter all she remembers is coming to on Margaret's living room floor with a cold, wet cloth pressed to her forehead.

Sheriff Johnsey pulled off a paved highway to access a dirt road. He could find his way to the Forked Deer River if he were blindfolded at high noon or one minute past midnight. This had been his spot since he and his brother were kids and their old man taught them the ways of the river. They swam, cooked out, shot pistols and of course fished this very spot the same way Sheriff Johnsey's dad did when he was a kid and probably his dad's dad as well. This and law enforcement had become rites of passage for the Johnsey men. His dad was a highway patrolman for thirty-five years and his brother, Hayes, was still on the force in Bristol, Tennessee. David disappointed and nearly broke his heart and other family members too when he chose investment banking over the badge. In retrospect, he had raised his son to be his own man and as crazy as things are today, physically and financially, he made the right decision.

Once Sheriff Johnsey passed mile marker 132 on the highway, the scent of the river lay heavy upon the air. His headlights cut through the haze of pre-morning and when he accelerated a whirlwind of debris chased after him. He knew every bend and bank, pit, and pothole on this narrow stretch of dirt road, intuitively maneuvered and navigated them all. He skidded to a stop, killed the headlights, emerged from his truck beneath a cloud of dust and slammed the door.

A single drop of daybreak fell into the valley, spread waves of pale gray light across the September landscape. He rattled fishing gear and folding chairs in the back of the pick-up and by the time he'd grabbed one in each hand, he'd awakened crickets, birds and an owl who winked one eye at a dissipating moon. At six thirty in the morning, the trees, stripped of their leaves, looked like giant stick men walking upon the earth.

Sheriff Johnsey made his way to the water's edge, opened two chairs and set them side by side. He sat in the chair on the left, primed two rods and reels with floats, weights, hooks. He laid one pole in the chair next to him.

"Alright, Alex. What's it going to be?" He smiled at the empty chair. "Tell you what. Let's start with some live bait and then we'll move on to a lure. It's yellow with black eyes and the hook is hidden by strands of yellow hair at the bottom of it. I hardly miss with that one."

Sheriff Johnsey opened the tackle box at his feet, removed the lid from a coffee can full of red worms. "I'm pretty good with these suckers too,' he laughed, holding one up that wiggled against the cool morning air. "Dug 'em early this morning out in the backyard while the Missus was still snoring." He slapped his thigh, dropped the worm back into the can. "Dad blast it! I forgot to remember." He hurried back to the pickup, grabbed a jacket and the six pack off the front seat, his gun from the glove compartment. He zipped up as tight as he could against the elements, made sure the safety was on the weapon when he slid it into his pocket and walked back the way he came, six cans of beer swinging in his right hand.

Sheriff Johnsey stood between the two chairs, popped a tab and emptied alcohol into the earth. He tried to think of something to say and when he could not, he kicked at the dirt and poured out another shot. He put the can beside the tackle box, impaled a worm on a hook and cast the line into the river. He set rod and reel and the half empty can of beer in the chair next to him. He tensed, put his hand on his pistol when he heard something behind him. But after several minutes of cocking his head at a right angle, there came the familiar sound of small critters scurrying about their daily grind. Sheriff Johnsey baited his own hook, cast its fate upon the waters. He let out a long satisfying sound after he opened another beer and took a long swallow. He examined the label on the can, belched.

"Kind of cold out here, Alex. They say Chicago is the worst in the winter time, though." He sat back in his chair, propped his feet up on the tackle box. "But what the hell? October is just a few days away. Supposed to be like this. But its good weather. Any weather is good for fishing and I'll tell you another thing too," he glanced sideways at the chair, "this is one of the best fishing spots you'll find. Period."

Sheriff Johnsey tightened the slack in his line, took two more sips of beer. A patch of blue sky rose over the horizon and in a few minutes he would call it morning. "Man, I tell you, I've cut a hole in the ice and went fishing in Minnesota, which took some getting used to. Stood in the middle of a clear stream in Montana and did some fly fishing. That's still beautiful every time I think about it. I've even been deep sea fishing off the Keys, which was tiresome. Fish was bigger and stronger than I was. But of all those places and all the others I haven't fished yet, I wouldn't trade this place for any of them. These waters," he pointed his index finger at the river, "may not be the cleanest or the biggest, but these waters run through my veins. They have laughed when I've laughed, counted my tears and dried them on this here bank. They know my secrets and refuse to tell them. And I know things about this river too. I know it has healing power if you have faith and wade in it. But if you disrespect its power and strength, it'll make a believer out of you. Every year, me and the rescue team pull at least one body out of these waters." Sheriff Johnsey belched. "I tell you Alex . . ."

He took another swallow when the rod and reel in the chair next to him thudded to the ground and was snaking towards the river. Sheriff Johnsey dropped everything, overturned his chair when he ran after and pick up the fishing pole. "Hold 'im, Alex," he shouted, struggling with the pole that was bent as if it were about to snap or would never be straight again. He pulled up the tip of the rod, reeled with such alacrity he thought his wrist would fall off, all the while dropping the tip back down. "Goddam, Alex. You're a natural. You been out here twenty minutes and you've got one of the biggest cats I've seen in awhile."

He took three steps backward. He could feel the fish's fight fading. "He's yours now, Alex. Reel 'im on in." The sun dug it heels into the wind, rose against the eastern sky and perched atop a cypress. When Sheriff Johnsey pulled the ten-pound catfish out of the water, it was gasping and golden in the brilliant light. "Alright, Alex. We got all day and we got more beer."

Sheriff Johnsey kneeled, removed the hook from the side of the fish's mouth and eased it back into the muddy water. He stood, shielded his eyes against the sun and watched the fish carry the river downstream.

About the Author

Image by: Minor Reed

JAMES E CHERRY is the author of five books: a collection of short fiction, a novel and three volumes of poetry. His latest collection of poetry, Loose Change, was published in 2013 by Stephen F. Austin State University Press. His prose and poetry has been featured in numerous journals and anthologies both in the U.S. as well as in England, France, China, Canada and Nigeria. He has been nominated for an NAACP Image Award, a Lillian Smith Book Award and was a finalist for the Next Generation Indie Book Award for Fiction. Cherry has an MFA in creative writing from the University of Texas at El Paso. He lives in Tennessee with his wife, Tammy.

Visit: http://www.jamesecherry.com.